The Cupid Caper

Port Provident: Holiday Hearts

Kristen Ethridge

I0619513

Dear Reader

I CAN'T LIE.

There's a lot of me in Amanda Marsh. I'm an English major and one of my favorite college classes was an entire semester on Shakespeare.

And obviously, I think there's something pretty special about love. I mean...I could write post-apocalyptic thrillers. (Actually, no, I couldn't.) But instead, I choose to write romance. I get to spend every day working toward a goal of happily-ever-after.

I had so much fun writing The Cupid Caper and going back to the halls of high school and creating a fun time to bring people together. I hope you'll enjoy your trip to the halls of Port Provident High School and that you'll find yourself smiling as you get to know Amanda and Luke. (And get to know Amanda's best friend, Lisa Fleming, as her story is coming next!)

I'd like to invite you to join me in Port Provident as we celebrate holidays and happily-ever-after this year with the Port Provident: Holiday Hearts series. Keep up with all the stories on my newsletter at www.kristenethridge.com[1]. You can also

---

1. http://www.kristenethridge.com

follow me on BookBub[2] to receive new release alerts every time a new book comes out.

All the best-

PS... I'D LIKE TO INVITE you to become a part of my reader community today. Just go to www.kristenethridge.com. You'll see the box to join right at the top of the page.

One of my signature Sweet Escape Romances is Layla and Ridge's story, *A Place to Find Love*. Layla's spent her whole life searching for a greater meaning in her life. She comes to Port Provident running on fumes, but once she meets Ridge, she begins a journey that fills her with more than she ever hoped for—faith, family, and a place to find the love she's always longed for. I'll send you a copy just for joining my reader community, plus you'll be able to keep up with the latest on my books and Port Provident through regular emails and more reader bonuses.

I promise these stories will lift you up and leave you with a smile.

One of the best ways to get to know Port Provident even better is to get your *Passport to Port Provident*. It's a behind-the-scenes reader exclusive that's available when you join me on Facebook Messenger[3].

---

2.   https://www.bookbub.com/authors/kristen-ethridge
3.   https://m.me/KristenEthridgeBooks

www.kristenethridge.com[4]
Facebook[5] Pinterest[6] Twitter[7] Instagram[8]
The Port Provident Community Center[9]

---

4. http://www.kristenethridge.com

5. https://www.facebook.com/KristenEthridgeBooks

6. http://www.pinterest.com/kethridgebooks/

7. https://twitter.com/kristenethridge

8. https://instagram.com/kristenethridge

9. https://www.facebook.com/groups/2422381554654795

Chapter One

"SO, WHAT ARE YOU GOING to do now that the cat's out of the bag?" Lisa Fleming leaned against the doorway of Amanda Marsh's classroom, her grin as feisty as another type of feline, the Cheshire Cat.

Amanda put down her red pen down and peered over the top of her glasses. "I have a thousand papers to grade before this weekend and you come to gossip?"

"Me? Gossip? I wouldn't dream of such a thing." Lisa feigned shock. "But tell me, Miss Shakespeare Teacher, what are you going to dream about when Luke Baker takes a leave of absence after Spring Break to go work on curriculum development for the new STEM Academy and then moves over there permanently next year?"

Port Provident ISD's new STEM Academy was the talk of the local education world. When it opened next fall, it would bring together the best teachers from across the district to teach Science, Technology, Engineering, and Mathematics to girls in a comprehensive format from Kindergarten through twelfth grade.

It would also take chemistry teacher Luke Baker away from the hallways of Port Provident High School and the daydreams of Port Provident's junior and senior level English teacher.

"I'm grading Lisa. Hush." She picked up her red pen. Maybe if she looked like she was focused on the piles of papers in front of her, Lisa would quit torturing her like a character from that *Mean Girls* movie.

"No you're not. That's *People* magazine on your desk. Not some AP test prep essay. You can't fool me." Lisa walked into Amanda's classroom and sat atop one of the desks in the back, near Amanda's own desk. "I know you got the email."

No use denying that. The announcement about the STEM Academy curriculum leads came out almost an hour ago, before the start of fourth period. "I did. And really, I'm happy for Luke. It's what he's wanted to do."

"Too bad all you've wanted to do for the past three years is go on a date with him."

"That is not accurate." Amanda could feel the tell-tale prickling in her cheeks, and knew she was beginning to blush the same color as the pen in her hand.

Lisa raised one eyebrow.

"It's only been two years," Amanda mumbled as she grabbed an essay off the pile at the corner of her desk. "He hasn't been at the school three years."

"Touché. My point still remains."

"I guess I'm going to do what anyone does when the—ahem—object of their affections moves on. I'll just move on too." Amanda tried to throw some sarcastic syllables in as she did her best to sound strong in her convictions. If she was honest with herself, she needed convincing far more than Lisa did. "Besides, you know I am just not in to that whole dating scene. There are no more fairy tales anymore."

"Really?" Lisa drew out the syllables. Amanda knew she was being baited.

"You know it and I know it. So, do you have any better ideas?"

"As a matter of fact, I do." Lisa stood up and pointed to the hand-painted poster from Student Council on the back wall. "You're just going to have to do what every other girl in this school is doing for the next week. The Cupid Caper."

"The Cupid Caper? Really, Lisa. I'm not eighteen. And I'm not participating in some secret Valentine scavenger hunt type thing—I mean, what is it, really, anyway?—to ask Luke Baker to a high school dance." The blush dropped from her cheeks like the mercury in a thermometer pelted by a cold front. "I should have known the resident drama teacher would have some kind of so-called solution with absolutely no basis in reality."

Lisa quickly closed the gap between her and the teacher's desk as she talked.

"Look, Amanda. Being the drama teacher means I can see through people's masks. I know when someone's pretending. And you're pretending like you don't care that Luke is leaving in a matter of a few weeks." She placed her hands squarely on the fake wood grain top of her best friend's desk. "Pretending poorly, I might add. You certainly aren't going to win an Oscar with this performance."

"I don't want to win an Oscar. I might like to win a date with Luke Baker. And still keep my dignity. But if I have to choose, I'll take my dignity every time."

Amanda looked at the industrial clock on the wall, narrow black hand marking the passage of each second. *Was her conference period over yet?*

Some break this was. Amanda coveted the thirty minutes of peace and quiet she got in the middle of each school day. Usually she filled the time with grading or polishing lesson plans. But the key was always peace and quiet.

Not today.

"I know you think I'm crazy. But you've had a crush on this guy for years, and now he's taking a new job at a new school. If you don't do something, you'll never see him again. Don't you think you ought to do *something*?"

Maybe Lisa was right. But if she made the wrong move, the gossip would spread like wildfire through the hallways of Port Provident High. And if there was anything more stressful than teaching about one-hundred-and-twenty seventeen- and eighteen-year-olds to love literature that wasn't necessarily on their Kindle, it was trying to teach those one-hundred-and-twenty seventeen-and eighteen-year-olds while they were laughing at her.

"I just don't think The Cupid Caper is the right answer. I know all the kids have a lot of fun with it, but I'm a teacher. It would be silly."

Lisa continued leaning over the desk, invading Amanda's personal space. Clearly, she thought she knew best, and she wasn't giving up. "Linda and Bob do The Cupid Caper every year, so there's precedent. Besides, insanity is defined as doing the same thing the same way and expecting different results, right?"

"Linda and Bob have been married for more than thirty years." The two math teachers were close to retirement and the unofficial grandparents to almost every teenager who walked the halls of Port Provident High. "And yes, it is. I tell my students that often."

"So..." A bright gleam twinkled in Lisa's eye. Amanda knew grand plans swirled in her best friend's head. And she knew she'd have to do some quick thinking to get them diffused. "Sometimes you just have to take Cupid's bow and arrow into your own hands."

"DR. BAKER?" THE OTHER students had raced out of the room when the final bell for the day rang, but Violet Clark lingered near the doorway.

"What's up, Violet?" Luke Baker pinched the center ring of a three-ring binder closed, then looked up at the shy girl with the dark curls.

"Is it true that you're leaving?" Apprehension spread clearly across her face. From the furrowed brow, to the dark stare, to the gentle chew on her lower lip, it was clear she'd heard the news somewhere—and it wasn't sitting well.

Although the announcement had been made to only faculty and staff a few periods before, it didn't surprise Luke one bit that word had gotten out to the kids. Information was the key commodity in the halls of any high school. Traded more furiously than stocks on Wall Street, there were no secrets that could be kept long.

"It's true. I'm headed to the new STEM Academy."

"But they said you're leaving before the year is over." The volume level of Violet's voice dialed sharply downward.

Luke could have kicked himself. In all the excitement of getting the call notifying him of his new position, he'd glossed over the part about telling his students. Most of them wouldn't necessarily care too much. Teachers came and teachers went. These kids rotated between seven classes a day. They were used to change, and as a whole, kids were resilient.

But still, there were some for whom attachments ran deep. And Violet Clark was one of them. The only child of a single mom who worked two jobs, Violet had blossomed in the chemistry lab. She'd found a world of rules and order, where things always made sense. A place where the giants like Marie Curie inspired young scientists even today with the promise of discovery.

And now, Violet had made a discovery which would change a very important corner of the world—the only secure corner she really possessed.

"Well, I don't know who *they* are..." Luke hesitated just a bit, wondering if he should try and soften it or just come out and lay out the truth. "But that's right. There will be a long-term sub in here after Spring Break. I'm being sent back to school in a way, myself. I'll be taking some courses that pertain to curriculum development. Then I'm going to spend most of the summer heading up the committee to bring together the curriculum we'll be using at the STEM Academy."

Violet nodded. "Can I come with you?"

Luke fiddled with the pen in his hand. He wasn't quite sure where she was going with this. "Where?"

"The STEM Academy."

Of course, Luke. The school. He needed to quit listening to the women in the teachers' lounge talking about students having crushes on teachers and all that stuff. Besides, Violet wasn't that type. If he didn't know himself better, he'd wonder if he'd been sniffing chemicals from the back cabinet of his chemistry lab.

"Well, there's an application process." Seeing the serious look that crossed her face, Luke made a decision. Violet was the type of girl who the STEM Academy catered to. Her whole life could be changed with exposure to the sciences and the higher-paying jobs she could have access to after college. "I'll print out a copy for you and we can work on the application together. There are some essays too."

Violet gave a shy smile. Luke felt good about making the offer. He'd spent time with a drug manufacturer before walking away to teach. No patent, no accolade, nothing in his former career gave him the same satisfaction as seeing the spark in a student's eyes.

"Maybe Miss Marsh could help me with those. Do you think she would?"

Luke wanted to say yes, but he didn't really know. Amanda Marsh always seemed to have a full plate. The students loved her English classes, and when she didn't have her nose in one of the classics, she was running to English department faculty meetings or working with the drill team. There were twenty-four hours in every day, and as best he could tell, Amanda Marsh scurried through every single one of them.

Quite frankly, he'd never seen the lights in her classroom off when he walked to his car—even late at night. He assumed she kept a futon in the back corner not for students to read, but so she could just sleep there and never leave.

"You could always ask her, Violet."

"I'll have to remember to do it tomorrow. I'm going to miss the bus if I don't hurry."

Luke gestured with his hands, a pushing motion toward the hallway. "Don't miss the bus. The applications aren't due for another two weeks. We'll get it taken care of."

"Ok, Dr. Baker. Thanks." Violet adjusted her backpack on her shoulders and turned to walk through the doorway. "I'll see you tomorrow."

"No problem, Violet. See you tomorrow."

Luke walked down the quiet hallway toward the doors which led to the teachers' parking lot at the back of the building. School ended about ninety minutes before, and without the jam-packed bustle of teenagers, Port Provident High seemed more in line with his old life at a corporate giant. People kept to themselves, just trying to finish the last of the day's work so they could go home.

The students gave the walls and halls their heart, and even though Luke believed deeply in the order and rules of chemistry and the sciences, he knew the energy he got from these kids more than made up for what was missing out of his paycheck these days.

He could see the light on in the room at the end of the hallway. A faux thatched roof poked out from over the doorway and construction paper timbers framed it. Amanda Marsh took her responsibility to literature seriously—down to decorating the entrance to her classroom to resemble Shakespeare's Globe Theatre.

Since she was still here, Luke decided to walk through the entrance to Shakespeare World and ask about the application essays on Violet's behalf. That way they could start working on them as soon as possible.

"Amanda? You got a minute?" Luke opened the door quietly and stepped inside.

A Tiffany-style lamp sat on the corner of Amanda's desk. It put a soft glow on her head, bent low tending to some of her grading. The light fell softly and gave her red hair highlights that sparkled like they could be measured in karats.

Amanda Marsh was one of those teachers everyone talked about—in a good way. Luke had always thought she was a bit scatterbrained, but as she lifted her head, light gray-green eyes upturned and a smattering of freckles across the bridge of her nose, Luke took a hard look at her.

And that look hit him hard right back, a punch to the gut.

It made him swallow hard, a roughness like sandpaper sliding down his throat. He'd worked with her for two years and had always thought of her as being Port Provident's own personal Lucy Ricardo.

Maybe he'd been wrong to stereotype her. Those eyes were serious, studying the words in front of her with intensity. And that hair. Soft, layered gently over her shoulders, and sassy.

Cut it out, Baker. He'd come in here to ask a favor from a colleague on behalf of a student. Not to ask the English teacher out on a date.

"Sure. What's up?" She'd looked up, but spoke before she really noticed who she was talking to. Her eyes flicked up to Luke's face, then immediately darted down toward the papers scattered across the desktop.

Scratch all that earlier stuff. The English teacher definitely was a scatterbrain. She couldn't even sustain eye contact.

"Hey, Violet Clark is in one of your classes, right?" He decided to stay back by the door. If scatterbrained-ness was catching, he didn't want to come down with a case. Luke was pretty sure none of his former colleagues back at Global Health were researching a vaccine for over-taxed synapse disorder.

Amanda lifted her head back and appeared to be squaring her jaw, as though she was fighting her way through something distasteful. Luke wished he'd never stopped by. He had a few degrees and some letters after his name that he didn't have much use for in a high school setting—sure they were in chemistry, but he'd had to write both a thesis and a dissertation. It wasn't like he didn't grasp the basics of the English language. Maybe he should just help Violet with the essays too.

"She's in my Advanced Placement English III class. Why do you ask?"

Luke decided to just throw it all out there bluntly, and get this over with. "She's expressed an interest in applying to the STEM Academy. I told her I'd help her with the overall application, but that there were some essays. She thought you might be able to review those for her."

Her ring finger tapped in a non-sensical pattern atop the stack of papers. "Sure. Violet's one of my best students in that class, though. I doubt she'll need much help."

"She's a good kid—does well in my class also. That's why I told her I'd help. I'll have her stop by once she's finished the essays. Should be later this week."

Luke turned to walk out the door, but before he could get back to the hallway, Amanda called out.

"Luke?" Her high, clear voice cut through the silence in the classroom like a diamond on glass.

He pivoted on the ball of his foot. "What?"

"The STEM Academy isn't exactly close to here. Violet's mother works too many hours to transport her over there. And they can't afford a car for Violet, even though I know she got her license last spring. Even if she got in to the new school, how will she get there every day?"

The nervousness on her face fell away, replaced with the soft shades of concern. Her lips fell a shade more pale, the freckles muted their orange shine, and the irises of her eyes shifted from mostly green to an overcast gray.

Clearly, Amanda Marsh cared as deeply for the quiet girl from the disadvantaged background as much as Luke himself did. He understood why. The young woman was a dream student: curious, conscientious, and respectful. Not every kid possessed those qualities in combination these days. Most had one or two, but the seasoned teachers around the halls said they wished they could teach one hundred Violet Clarks.

"You know," Luke said slowly, trying to think of something he could do to change the reality of the situation. "I don't know, Amanda."

She raked a hand through her shiny hair and let out a deep breath. "I love the idea of the STEM Academy, but I worry about kids like Violet who would thrive in that environment—but can't get there. I'm just not sure we're doing the right thing as a district. Maybe we should have focused on creating programs within the existing schools."

"I think the STEM Academy is still the right move." He tried not to be defensive, but he took the STEM Academy personally. He'd been one of the key employees in the district backing this project. If the STEM Academy failed students before even getting off the ground—well, it was like *he* failed students.

And he didn't get into teaching to fail his students.

"I'm sure it is. Even this English teacher thinks a place with a higher focus on science and math and those career paths is a great idea. I just worry about the kids like Violet—all of the talent to really benefit from it, but lacking the support and resources to make the transition."

Luke nodded. He felt like he was reassuring himself as much as the English teacher. "It'll work."

Chapter Two

NO ONE EVER ACCUSED Amanda of being a morning person, but the students always expected an A-game from their teachers. So, just as she did every morning, Amanda sipped a Venti latte with an extra shot of espresso that she bought from the designer coffee shop just around the corner from the high school. She didn't necessarily like pushing a five-dollar-bill through the drive through window every morning, but it made her twitch just a little bit to think about what would happen if she changed her morning routine and *didn't* make the stop.

As she straightened up the papers on her side table, a familiar voice called out as Lisa stepped through the doorway to the Globe Theatre and into Amanda's classroom.

"Good morning, Sunshine!"

Amanda couldn't stop her eyes from rolling. "I left the house before the sun got up this morning and Mr. Pickles smirked at me as he buried back in the blankets."

"Mr. Pickles is a cat. Of course he smirked. That's the official facial expression of cats everywhere. He and that Grumpy Cat from the Internet are brothers from another feline mother."

"That's the truth." Amanda couldn't help but laugh.

The petite drama teacher walked toward her friend with an over-exaggerated sideways step. "Sooooo?"

Amanda waved her hands, mocking her friend's attempts at stealth. "Sooooo what?"

"So did you think more about doing The Cupid Caper?"

Although she couldn't exactly put words to a description of the hopeful, crazy smile on Lisa's face, she could put the exact words to her answer.

"No."

"You didn't think about it? So there's still hope?" Lisa executed a small twirl on the industrial blue carpet.

"No, I didn't think about it. And no, there's no hope. The answer is no, for all of it." Amanda walked over to her computer and pulled up her email. "And the bell's going to ring in just a bit. Shouldn't you be heading back to the drama cave?"

"I just think you're making a mistake, Amanda. Why not have a little fun?"

Amanda placed a hand defiantly on her hip, feeling vaguely like she should start singing the "I'm a little teapot..." song.

"Because there's nothing fun about embarrassing myself in front of a colleague."

Lisa wouldn't back down. Her dogged determination was the antithesis of Mr. Pickles and his lazy sneer earlier today. "For not even four more weeks. Then he's moving on. And you'll never have to see him again. And you don't even work with him now. He's on the science faculty. They're on the second floor, in the opposite corner of the building. You see him at monthly staff meetings. Of which we only have one left before he goes off into the wide world of curriculum planning."

"Lisa, quit it. Really. I just don't want to. I teach stories about love. I just don't believe in it much anymore and you know that. Besides, I am working with him on a project."

"Like what?" Lisa's tone clearly said she thought Amanda was not being truthful.

"Violet Clark wants to apply to the STEM Academy. He's helping her with her application and I'm going to look over her essays. Not that she needs help from either of us—she's the smartest kid I've taught in years."

The slightly puzzled look didn't fall from Lisa's face. "How did this come about?"

"He stopped by here yesterday after school to let me know Violet was interested in my help."

"Luke Baker came by your room yesterday to ask for your help on a project?"

"Yes." Amanda's hand returned reflexively to her hip. "What?"

Amanda cocked an eyebrow as her head nodded slowly. "Interesting."

"No, Lisa. Just part of the job. I'm afraid it's not going to work, anyway."

The eyebrow inched even further toward Amanda's high hairline. "How so?"

"I don't see how Violet's going to be able to get to the STEM Academy. She doesn't have a car and her mother can't afford one. And her mother already works two jobs as it is. She wouldn't be able to take Violet across town." It hurt just thinking about denying an opportunity to a student of Violet's potential just because of something as simple as a car.

"The Cupid Caper." Lisa said the words slowly, and with conviction.

"Lisa, for the last time, I said no."

Lisa shook her head with all the force of a strong gale-force wind. "Not you."

"Not me? Then who?" Amanda couldn't tell what her friend was getting at. She'd heard a lot of hare-brained things come out of Lisa's mouth. She could usually keep up with her best friend's tangents—a second-hand, common language was part of being a best friend, after all—but this time, Amanda was baffled.

"Violet." Lisa said the name matter-of-factly, as though it should have been obvious.

"Violet? In The Cupid Caper? Why?"

Lisa's face lifted into a wide grin. "Don't you remember? Kittrick Motors donated a one-year car lease as the grand prize."

Amanda had actually forgotten all about any of the prizes. She turned over the Student Council sponsor reins at the end of the last school year, so she honestly hadn't kept up with the ins-and-outs of The Cupid Caper, which served as the Student Council's main fundraiser for the spring semester.

"That's great, Lisa, but it still doesn't solve the problem. Violet's mom is pretty strict. I doubt she lets her even go to the Valentine's dance. And where is Violet going to get the money to pay the taxes on the prize?"

"The lease was donated to the school. The Student Council is a non-profit. The dealership takes the deduction."

The skepticism wouldn't leave the pit of Amanda's stomach. If, somehow, there was a way for Violet to win the use of that car for a year, that would indeed solve the problem. But there was no way to count on her winning the grand prize.

Especially if Violet's mother wouldn't let her have anything to do with The Cupid Caper or the Valentine's dance.

"Ok. But we can't exactly rig the drawing for Violet to win. It's all chance." Amanda could feel the disappointment coming through in her voice.

"Not this year, it's not." Lisa's smile got even more profound. "You haven't been paying attention. This year, it's not a raffle drawing. The students are going to vote for a winner based on the couples who complete The Cupid Caper challenge. The Student Council picks the finalists, then the students have a vote at the dance."

"But I told you, I don't see any way Violet's mom lets her participate. And I don't even think Violet is interested in any boys to ask to the dance anyway."

The first bell rang, the tinny sound reverberating through the cheap speaker in the ceiling.

Lisa gave another wobbly pirouette, then headed for the door. "We're covering Method Acting today in my Intro to Drama Class."

"And?" Amanda had lost count of the number of Lisa's rabbit trails this morning. She couldn't keep up with her crazy friend's mental wanderings.

"Fake it until you make it, honey. There's always a way."

Lisa disappeared out the doorway, but Amanda shouted behind her. "I don't get it."

"You will, my dear. You will."

Somewhere in Lisa's world, that was probably meant to be reassuring. But Amanda knew it would just leave her trying to figure out riddles all day.

THE DAY SEEMED TO DRAG on, long past the normal length of a school day. Luke could feel the minutes on the clock weighing him down. He honestly hadn't felt this way in three years, since that bitter January he decided he was leaving his lab at Global Health and not looking back. Today, he supposed the crawling passage of time indicated a change just around the corner.

The honest truth simply came down to this: now that Luke knew the curriculum lead job was his, he couldn't wait to get started. He loved his kids here at Port Provident and would miss teaching them greatly—hopefully some, like Violet Clark, would be in his classes at the STEM Academy—but he felt energized by the challenge ahead and couldn't wait to get started.

Getting kids interested in the sciences, technology, and mathematics excited him. He knew first-hand the importance of having the right teachers and the right lessons to spark that interest and make that life-long connection.

It spoke to his sense of adventure to be that guide for young minds. He liked ziplining through the Brazilian rainforest and SCUBA diving off the Great Barrier Reef, but he knew that kind of experience couldn't be had every day.

Watching the fire in a teenager's eyes as they connected with something life changing? It's why he changed his career path to teaching.

He'd been to every continent—even Antarctica—but no check on the bucket list, no rush of adrenaline came close to serving as a student's mentor.

"Hey Dr. B." Kinley McDonald walked through the open door. Sixth period was his conference time, so the usual low-pitched hum of the chemistry lab was silent for twenty-five more minutes.

"Kinley, what's up?" Luke swiveled the tall blue chair behind his lecture stand-level desk toward the girl.

"I'm just delivering envelopes for The Cupid Caper." She held out a brown basket stuffed with red and white notes.

The Cupid Caper. One of the silliest traditions of the year at Port Provident High. Students would pay an entry fee to the Student Council, then go chasing after their secret crush. There would be riddles, miniature scavenger hunts, and gifts. In the end, if you guessed your suitor, you got special recognition at the Valentine's Day dance and were eligible to win some big prize.

All in all, it made Luke very glad to be past his own teenage years. He'd attended most of the dances at his alma mater, but he generally preferred the route of just asking the girl out directly.

He liked a good adventure, but romantic espionage wasn't Luke's thing.

"That time of year again, huh?" Luke tried to keep the sarcasm out of his voice. "Do you need my help with something?"

"Nope." Kinley's ponytail bobbed and swayed as she shook her head. "I've got one for you."

She dug in the basket, pulled out a red envelope, and held out her hand.

"You what?"

Luke could feel a smattering of wetness on his lips. He'd definitely sputtered out his response. Great. That was just about as undignified as The Cupid Caper itself.

"Congrats there Dr. B. You're the first teacher I've ever seen get picked. Well, except for Mr. and Mrs. Wallace." Kinley waggled the envelope in front of her teacher, imploring him to take it. "Oh, and don't worry. It's not a student. Mrs. Langton wouldn't let that happen. It's an adult."

He raked a hand savagely through his hair. "That's supposed to make me feel better?"

"Well, it'd be kinda creepy otherwise, Dr. B." She stepped forward and laid the card on the corner of his desk when it became apparent that Luke was not going to take the envelope for himself.

Luke let out a short sigh. "That it would, Kinley. What am I supposed to do with it?"

"Open it up and read it. This year, they're supposed to be written in haiku. The poem should give you the first hint about your secret admirer."

"Haiku." There was no way those two syllables could have come out any more flat.

"The good ol' five-seven-five."

"What?" He'd gotten pretty good with the crazy made up words teenagers these days used—or so he thought, until right this moment.

"Syllables, Dr. B. A haiku is a poem made up of three lines. The first is five syllables, the second is seven syllables, and the third is five again." She spoke matter-of-factly, as though all chemistry Ph.D.s should have known this secret to the universe.

"And this is supposed to be romantic?"

Luke felt like Alice through the looking glass. The whole thing just seemed curiouser and curiouser.

"No. Actually it's supposed to be kinda annoying. You've gotta work for this date."

Luke raised his right eyebrow. "I have never worked for a date to a high school dance in my life."

Kinley smiled, a touch of mirth taking over her entire face. "Well, then, it's time you lightened up, Dr. B. You know what they say—you only live once."

Oh no. He'd been YOLOed. "Um, thanks, Kinley."

"You're welcome, Dr. B. I've gotta go deliver the rest of these. Later."

She ducked out of the room as quietly as she'd entered, leaving Luke alone with a closet full of chemicals and an envelope full of haiku.

He didn't know which would kill him the fastest.

He flicked the offensive envelope a bit with his finger. He didn't really want to find out what lurked inside.

"Five-seven-five. YOLO." Luke pushed his hand through his hair again. "No-LO."

Determined not to open the small red rectangle, he pushed it even further to the side. It dangled precariously over the wastebasket.

One more little nudge and he'd be hai-through with this haiku business.

"Wait. You got a Cupid Caper poem?" Amanda Marsh's jaw dropped a little as she took in the scene before her.

"Is that impossible for you to imagine?" Luke thought he should be insulted by the insinuation, but he wasn't sure why he cared. It bothered him a little, like a shirt tag that wouldn't lay flat.

Amanda lifted her hand and waved an identical red envelope. "The Student Council Postmaster made it by my room too."

"It's a haiku, I hear." Luke felt a little better about the skeptical look on her face. They both seemed to share the same opinion of the mail.

Amanda rolled her eyes, the gentle green in the middle edging out the duskier shades around the edges. "You didn't send this to me, did you?"

Luke opened his mouth to say the first thing that came to mind, then stopped himself. No sense finding out if the rumors about red-headed tempers were true. He stopped himself, eyes locked on the woman in front of him. She wore a cotton knit shirt with a neckline that grazed the collarbone. Trim and tailored, the shirt fit and flared along every curve.

The fact that it was the same Valentine red as the envelope in question sent off his own internal siren. He needed to get a grip before the English teacher—or anyone else who might walk in the room—realized he was checking her out.

"Well, did you send this to me?" He averted his eyes downward and flicked at the envelope again. It fell into the wastebasket, landing atop the pile of crumpled papers with a satisfying slap.

"Of course not," she bit out with lightning speed.

"Methinks the lady doth protest too much."

"You know, *Hamlet*," the English teacher aimed the Danish prince's name squarely at the man behind the modern chemistry desk. "In Shakespeare's day, a protest was not what we think of now—it wasn't a complaint. The Elizabethans used protest to mean a vow. So when Queen Gertrude says 'The lady doth protest too much, methinks,' she's actually saying the woman looks like she's over-promising, not necessarily over-denying. Of course, Hamlet turns that back on his insincere mother."

Luke leaned back slightly in his tall chair. "Interesting. I didn't realize that."

Amanda nodded. "The phrase has evolved to mean something else, as language so often does. I find it fascinating how words change through time."

What Luke found fascinating was the passion written across Amanda's face. Her eyes sparkled with bright glitter, the apples of her cheeks glowed a dusty pink, and her features fully animated as she talked.

He'd mentally made fun of her Globe Theatre doorway for the last two years. But now he saw it in a completely different light.

Amanda Marsh hadn't decked the entry to her classroom out to look like the world's most famous theatre because she possessed an arts-and-crafts streak gone awry, as he'd always assumed. She turned her classroom into Shakespeare's world because she wanted to bring the literature she loved alive in tangible ways for her students.

He found that outlet in chemistry lessons—solutions mixing, Bunsen burners lighting, test tubes and beakers holding experiments as they took shape. She found it in words, in the alchemy of personal expression.

"What?" She took half a step back from where she'd stood and the fire that had lit her face just moments before burned down to the dusty embers of self-consciousness and wariness.

"Nothing."

That word's meaning hadn't changed through the centuries, but the chemistry teacher knew without a doubt that he doth protest too much, in a completely modern sense of the phrase.

"If you say so."

Luke could tell Amanda wasn't convinced.

Her implication that he was thinking something through was completely spot-on. But there was no way he was sharing the thoughts in his mind with her. She'd think he was crazy.

In all honesty, Luke thought he was a little crazy at this very moment. He'd worked under the same roof with Amanda for two years. They hadn't had much personal interaction, and what there'd been...well, he'd just never paid too much attention.

But starting with that trip to her classroom yesterday, everything changed. And now, he couldn't take his eyes off her. Clearly, she'd picked up on it too—so he wasn't even being subtle about it. He'd like to blame it on fumes in the lab.

Except there were no experiments going on in here.

Just the experiment in his mind where he wondered what it would be like to be someplace with dim lighting, candles, a glass of wine, and Amanda Marsh explaining the finer nuances of Shakespeare's sonnets to him.

Luke hopped out of the chair like a firecracker had been planted in the seat.

He had to get his mind back under control.

"Stupid Cupid," he muttered to himself.

"What?" Amanda laughed as she said the word, making the "a" in the middle drag out for several syllables.

Think fast, Baker.

Luke waved in the direction of the trash can, where the red envelope lay atop the heap of discards. "The Cupid Caper. If you didn't send that to me and I didn't send that to you, then what's going on?"

Amanda's eyes went round with mock surprise. "Oh, you *didn't* send this to me?"

"No. Of course not."

Amanda's eyes stayed broadly open, but they no longer conveyed surprise.

"I didn't mean that the way it sounded. I just meant that I don't do things like The Cupid Caper."

She tapped her envelope lightly against her leg. "Things like The Cupid Caper? You don't believe in fun? Or love? Or both?"

"Of course I believe in fun. What kind of guy do you think I am?"

He hadn't believed in love for a long time. But that was better left unsaid.

"I don't know, Luke. I mean, we work together, but I don't really know you." Amanda continued to play aimlessly with the red rectangle.

For some reason, her reply made the hair along the back of his neck prickle with the sense of a mild challenge. Before he'd had a chance to think further, he found himself meeting the test.

"Well, we could change that, you know."

"What?" There she went again, dragging out that vowel.

"Not knowing each other. How late are you going to be here tonight?"

Luke sniffed the air. Some student had to have left some jar open, some test tube uncapped. Stray chemicals had to be blamed for this.

Or pheromones. You know, they're your body's chemicals, Baker.

"Probably until about five o'clock. I've got a rehearsal with the drill team officers after school."

"Ok, then. I'll stop by your classroom at five. Will that work?"

"Yes, I guess so, but..." Amanda's thought trailed off. Luke could see her searching for the right words. "But it'll work for what, exactly?"

"Dinner." Luke sounded far more confident than he felt. He hadn't been on a date since he started teaching. Of course, that had initially been his own choice as he navigated the career transition. Then as the months passed, it turned into something else entirely.

Apathy.

Once he left Global Health, he'd discovered the rush of knowing your work made a difference. It had been the perfect complement to his sky-diving, rock-climbing, triathlon-completing adrenaline junkie ways.

And he'd decided he wasn't settling for anything less than that again.

Especially not in love.

Since he'd made that decision, Luke had never found anyone who stoked his curiosity like the lithe, red-headed English teacher started doing twenty-four hours ago.

He couldn't figure out why he'd *seen* her a thousand times before, but never *noticed* her.

"Did your haiku tell you to do this?" The skepticism slid back across her face like a mask.

"My haiku?"

"From The Cupid Caper. Are you sure you didn't send this?" She lifted the envelope up by her face. "You can be honest. If it was a joke, I'm a big girl. I can take it."

Luke closed the space between them with one step.

"It wasn't a joke." He could smell her perfume and decided the high, sweet floral notes had to be the most pleasant thing to ever come from a lab.

He balled up his fists and stuffed them in his pockets to keep himself from reaching out and wiping that uneasy look of Amanda's away.

"It wasn't a joke. And I don't take directives from haiku. I don't even know what it said."

She slid her envelope between them. "Open it."

Amanda's voice barely rose above a whisper.

Luke took one hand out of its pocket and grasped the red paper. He just barely grazed the top of her pointer finger with his own, but her softness sliding under the tip of his finger caused an undeniable chemical reaction inside his skin.

Pheromones. Definitely the pheromones. They poured out like foam-topped liquid on draft beer night at a baseball game.

Slowly, Luke leaned back and tugged the envelope open.

"The old class/A teacher goes in/The sound of kids." He read the syllables slowly, allowing his pulse the chance to do the same. "That's not five-seven-five."

Amanda tugged on the paper, angling it toward her. "No, it's a play on Basho's The Old Pond, the most famous haiku written. It goes 'The old pond/A frog goes in/The sound of water.'"

"O-o-okay. There's a reason I teach chemistry, I guess."

She smiled and the light returned to the smooth curves of her face. "Can we see what yours says?"

Amanda looked at the note discarded on the trash can, and Luke turned to go pluck it out. "Here you go. You do the honors."

She opened it carefully, but didn't say a word. Luke took it from her, and mentally chided himself at his realization that he'd hoped to brush her narrow fingers again.

"So much depends upon/The Cupid Caper/Glazed with hearts and flowers/Beside our favorite teachers."

Luke shook his head strongly. "That's not even a haiku."

"No. That's a play on William Carlos Williams' The Red Wheelbarrow. We covered it in my American Lit AP class last week. This has to be one of my students."

"Amanda, this whole Cupid Caper is strange enough to me, but I sure don't want some student flirting with me. Maybe we should just turn these in to Liz."

Liz Langton was the Assistant Principal who oversaw the Student Council, and therefore The Cupid Caper.

"Yeah, I agree. I'm not taking any chances."

"Give me yours and I'll take them both after school while you have your drill team meeting."

Amanda handed him her poem carefully, as though she could pick up cooties from the paper.

"Now, what were you stopping by for?" Luke had gotten so caught up in red envelopes—and red hair—that he'd never actually asked her why she'd come to the chemistry hallway.

"Oh, I wanted to talk with you a little more about Violet Clark."

Just then, the bell rang.

"Ok, well, that's our cue. We can talk about it tonight, though."

Amanda pursed her lips in thought. But as the hallway began to fill with student chatter, the only thoughts Luke had were definitely not educational.

Well, actually, maybe they were closer to the average high schooler's thoughts than he cared to admit.

"Tonight then. I'll see you after drill team."

"See you then."

As she stepped back through the doorway, Luke feared the only thing he'd see until five o' clock was the image of her lips, cotton candy pink and puckered up as though they were ready for a kiss.

A kiss he couldn't give a co-worker, no matter how many haikus sang Amanda Marsh's praises.

Chapter Three

THE TALK OF DRILL TEAM practice was everyone's Cupid Caper poems. The officers passed them around, squealed a little, and speculated on the meaning.

Not for the first time, Amanda noted that a teenager's ability to read too far into seventeen syllables was worthy of some sort of CIA-level detective work.

What shocked Amanda was how a certain grown adult she knew well couldn't stop from doing the same. If Luke Baker hadn't sent that poem, who had? She really hoped that it wasn't a student, because that would just be far too awkward. But since she'd taught both the Basho poem as part of a poetry unit at the beginning of the year, the logical conclusion brought her to believe she had to be someone's teenage crush. And then the fact that she'd just taught The Red Wheelbarrow not two weeks ago...well, she felt certain whoever was behind these poems was sitting in her class.

"Did you hear Ms. Pantego got a poem too?"

Amanda's ears perked up and she interjected herself into the girls' conversation without pause for thought. "A teacher got a poem?"

"Yeah." Schuyler Welch nodded her head, honey blonde ponytail bobbing along in agreement. "And she wasn't the only one."

Lindsay Moore jumped in next. "Nope. Four teachers got them. I put together some of the envelopes."

Four teachers? Then it probably wasn't a coincidence. Amanda held her breath a little bit, hoping Port Provident wasn't about to become a bad TV investigation special. They'd say that Port Provident High was a school straight from the pages of *Lolita*.

Her mind began to run faster than a roller coaster, up one side of the hill of absurdity, then careening down the back side, thoughts, speculation, and questions flying with wild abandon in the wake.

"So who is sending them?" Amanda tried to keep the tension out of her voice. She wanted to just play it cool. Sniff out the information. Then make a plan to take it back to Liz Langton and get it stopped before everything went too far.

"I can't tell you, Miss M." Lindsay crossed her arms in a gesture of wordless defiance.

"Lindsay. You have to tell me. If students are sending these to teachers, we can't have that. We've never had this many teachers get pulled in to The Cupid Caper. If something inappropriate is going on, we have to stop it."

The roller coaster in Amanda's mind continued to move.

"It's been approved."

Lindsay was a rule follower. She didn't have any problems doing just as she was told. Normally, Amanda regarded this as an admirable character trait, something every teacher wanted in a student.

But right this second, Amanda fervently wished Lindsay was a typical seventeen-year-old gossip. The drill team lieutenant knew more than she was letting on—that much was obvious.

And Amanda needed to know what Lindsay knew.

"I heard you got one too, Miss M." Schuyler couldn't hold back a saucy grin.

A low whistle came from Mary Beth Parker. "You go, girl."

Amanda put two fingers in her mouth and let out a whistle of her own. Shrill and forceful, the sound echoed off the shiny hardwood floors of the gym and stopped the girls in their tracks, just as she'd intended.

"Yes, I got one. And I think it came from a student. So I need to know what you girls know so we can straighten this out before it gets bad. You know me. And you know I'm not going to a dance with one of my students, not even as a joke. It wouldn't be right."

Hopefully she could make them see the issue clearly.

"Why do you think it came from a student?" Mary Beth sat down behind Schuyler and started to braid her friend's thick ponytail.

Amanda thought back to opening the red envelope in Luke's classroom. Although she hadn't really expected for him to admit to sending the poem, a part of her wished he hadn't been so dismissive of the idea.

Realistically, she knew he didn't reciprocate her crush on him.

But it would have been nice if he had.

But then again, he was stopping by her classroom in a few minutes. And they were going to go somewhere and talk about Violet Clark's application to the STEM Academy. She'd finally gotten her chance for time with Luke Baker away from campus.

But she knew it meant nothing more than two teachers trying to help a student.

And for someone whose life's calling was teaching, that should have been enough.

Too bad her heart spoke louder than her mind.

She remembered the words Luke had said earlier.

Stupid Cupid, indeed.

"Miss M.? We're waiting. Why do you think it came from a student?"

"Oh..." She'd been caught. Good thing the girls weren't mind readers. "Because both the poems were takes on poems I've taught in my classes."

"Both the poems?" Mary Beth stopped stuffing a T-shirt into her bag. "You got two? You have two Cupids?"

Oops.

Open mouth, insert jazz shoe-clad foot. She could feel a cramp poking at the ball of her big toe. The small knot of muscle fibers twitched slightly, then sent tendrils like spider's legs sliding through the surrounding tissue.

"No, thank goodness, I don't." Amanda pointed her foot, then flexed, then repeated the action slowly. She needed to work out that cramp. And some time to pull together her thoughts.

"Then what did you mean?" The girls all started talking over one another, as teenage girls in a group tended to do. Some days, Amanda wondered how she maintained her sanity. Today clearly was shaping up to be one of them.

First crafty poetry, then excitable high school girls.

And then the dinner she'd aimlessly daydreamed about for since new teachers were introduced at the first staff meeting of the year, two years ago...

But now that the day had arrived, she wasn't too sure about walking into her dream. Sometimes real life was just too...real.

That's why she liked literature so much.

What if she went out with Luke Baker, discovered he was completely boring, and realized that two years of daydreaming had been a waste?

Now that she was less than an hour away from getting what she'd thought about for two years, Amanda wondered if she shouldn't have just been content to be the Port Provident High School version of Walter Mitty, full of grand ideas and the lofty triumphs of the imagination.

"Hey, Miss M." Mary Beth tapped Amanda on the shoulder with an insistent finger. "You're totally zoned out."

"Oooh. Cupid's got her. She's thinking about her poems." Schuyler giggled.

"Poem," Amanda retorted. "I told you I only got one."

"Yeah, but you said 'both the poems.' That's two. Who got the other one?" The girls all closed in as Schuyler refused to let their drill team director off the hook.

"Dr. Baker got one too. We happened to be together when we opened them."

Schuyler's eyebrows lifted and she nodded her head, an impish smile on her face. "Dr. Baker's kinda hot." The other girls nodded in agreement.

"Girls. Stop." Amanda had to end this now. It was bad enough that she'd spent two years of faculty meetings staring at the back of his head and noticing the way his shoulders filled out his lightly-starched button down shirts perfectly. But knowing her drill team girls had basically done the same...ugh. She had to shut it down. For her own sake—and Luke's. He'd been bothered enough when they'd discussed the potential source of the poems. This wouldn't be well-received either.

"But Miss M. You kinda started it."

"Yeah, and I'm ending it. Just tell me what you know about these poems sent to teachers." Amanda waved her hands in front of her in the universal sign for "hush" as the girls started talking over one another again. "Lindsay. It's time to come clean. This really isn't funny. The Cupid Caper is supposed to be light-hearted, but we can't have students sending sonnets to teachers."

Lindsay looked around to make sure no one else had entered the gym. Just as Amanda suspected. The Student Council Vice-President knew more than she'd let on.

"They're not coming from students, Miss M." The matter-of-fact tone in her voice left no room for doubt or argument. Amanda knew Lindsay told the truth.

But the truth didn't make any sense.

"So where did they come from? Y'all said there were several teachers who got them." Amanda channeled her inner Sherlock Holmes. She was determined to get to the bottom of this.

"I don't know, exactly. Mrs. Langton signed off on it. When I received the forms, they had all been filled out in her handwriting. The buyer was listed as the Port Provident Baccheus Society."

The Roman god of wine? She knew Liz liked to go to the Wine Down Wednesday event that a local restaurant hosted weekly. So that part made sense. Too bad the rest of it really didn't.

That cramp in her foot seized up again. *Point. Flex. Point. Flex. Point. Try not to go crazy.*

"But I don't get it." For once, the English teacher had run out of eloquent words.

"No one does. But they all came in with a sizeable donation to The Cupid Caper, so the Student Council officers were all pretty glad."

Before Amanda could say anything further, Lindsay's cell phone rang. It vibrated loudly on the gym floor. "That's my mom. I'm supposed to be home by 4:30. Hey, Mary Beth, do you still need a ride?"

Mary Beth stood up and walked over to her bag. "Yeah, I do. Thanks."

The officers all stood up and disbursed, leaving Amanda alone in the silent gym. As she walked back to the private bathroom for faculty for a quick shower before heading back to her room, Amanda couldn't shake the threads that cluttered her mind like dusty cobwebs.

She now knew, from one of the coordinators of the event, that these notes were definitely not being sent from students to teachers.

But she also now knew they'd all been filled out by an assistant principal. And an assistant principal couldn't be running some kind of dating club for her employees.

None of it made any sense. Had Cupid picked up some of Baccheus' wine before he went out for target practice?

LUKE SAT ON TOP OF a table at the back of Amanda's classroom. He'd tried to wedge himself in between a stack of projects and another stack of textbooks. Surrounded by signs of education, he took the moment to do a little studying of his own.

Like studying the reasons he hadn't been able to get Amanda Marsh off his mind since this time yesterday. Luke couldn't pin down if his thoughts locked on repeat because she knew her way around a haiku or because she clearly cared as much about one of his favorite students as he did.

Or maybe it had something to do with the fact that she was the only redhead he'd ever seen that could carry off wearing fire-engine red.

And she was certainly the only redhead that sent sirens off in him like she did earlier today.

They'd worked under the same roof and taught the same students for two years. But in a matter of weeks, that would come to a quick end. He'd go to design curriculum at Spring Break and begin teaching at the STEM Academy in the fall.

And that's why he needed to pull the plug on all those sirens and lights. It couldn't go anywhere if they were teaching under the same roof. And it wasn't going to go anywhere if they weren't.

Luke promised himself he'd keep his emotions in check, enjoy dinner with a colleague, and see what they could come up with to help Violet.

And that was it.

"Sorry I'm running late." Amanda breezed into the room, her deep titian hair pulled into a loose ponytail at the nape of her neck. Some of the strands clung together with a gentle dampness that caused the loose waves she normally wore to twist a little more than usual.

Luke felt his resolve sprint away as quickly as a fire truck en route to a four-alarm call.

There were four alarms in his world, no doubt about that.

Pulse jumping.

Breathing quickening.

Adrenaline surging.

Mind wandering places it hadn't gone for a long time.

She'd clearly showered, but had chosen to dress back in the same clothes she'd worn earlier. The same bright red shirt, tailored neckline skimming from shoulder to shoulder, just at the edge of her ivory collarbones.

Luke's fingers itched a bit, jealous of the fabric.

He felt a little ridiculous, envying cherry-red cotton. But nothing about his reaction to Amanda made sense anymore.

"You're fine, don't worry about it." Luke wished the sentence applied to him. His pulse tapped harder, leaving a staccato in his veins as they criss-crossed his body. He knew he wasn't fine. And he worried if he ever would be again.

She opened the cabinet behind her desk and pulled out her purse and a bag filled with papers to grade. "Just once I'd love to leave this behind, you know?"

Luke knew. He'd like to leave his rational mind—the one which told him dinner had to be about helping Violet and nothing more—behind. "Well, why don't you?"

"Come on. You know why. If I don't stay on top of this grading, then it'll grow and grow and be the end of me."

The end of him was going to come quickly, if he didn't quit staring. Either his pulse would race him straight into the cardiac unit at the nearby hospital, or Amanda would notice his eyes locked on her and she'd slap him right back where he belonged.

And he wouldn't blame her one bit.

"Yeah, I remember being one of those smug corporate people who talked about teachers having their summers off. And then I became a teacher and I realized they needed three months off to make up for all the overtime of grading at night."

"That is truth being spoken right there. I love this job, but some nights, I'd just like to veg out in front of the TV." Amanda's eyes caught the fluorescent lighting overhead and twinkled a little as she smiled. She picked up her bag of grading, her purse, and a small gym bag. "You ready?"

"I am. Let me help you with that."

As Amanda came near, Luke reached out. He placed a hand on her shoulder to slow her down. He knew it wasn't possible, but he could almost feel the red cotton shirt burning his fingers where they landed on the gentle curve at the top of her arm.

Wordlessly, he slid the strap of the black gym bag to the edge of Amanda's shoulder, then slid it down her arm with the pressure of two fingers.

Amanda turned her head slightly and locked her gaze on Luke's. Her lips parted slightly and Luke heard a short breath pull in between them. She felt the charge in the air too.

The gym bag hit the floor with a soft thud. The sensible thing to do would have been to just grab it. But Luke didn't want to be sensible.

He'd lived by rules and order for his whole life. A love for science—where hypotheses were tested and laws explained why the sky was blue and why people didn't float off into space—had fed Luke's Type-A personality for more than three decades.

"Tell me..." He barely recognized his own voice.

Amanda never blinked, never closed that sigh-sized space between her lips. "What?"

"Tell me, what does your Mr. Shakespeare say about someone like me? Someone who believes in only what they can test, what they can see?"

Her voice formed the perfect counterpoint to his—soft where his had been rough—as the words pushed their way past the usual reserve that would have held the emotions securely back.

"'Love looks not with the eyes, but with the mind/And therefore is winged Cupid painted blind.'"

Something about the words she chose made sense. Luke's fingers still rested on her sleeve, just above the elbow. Maybe it was the physical connection.

Maybe it was something else. Maybe he should have paid more attention to The Bard.

"When did he say that?"

"*A Midsummer Night's Dream.*"

"And what do you say, Amanda Marsh? Do you believe all those words you teach students?"

She shifted a little and the change of position caused Luke's hand to drop back to his side.

"I believe in the sincerity of the people who wrote them. I believe in people who took that chance."

It seemed as though she spoke of something very personal, but something he knew nothing about. Her words felt guarded. On second thought, he knew all about staying guarded.

"Do you still want a chance to get to know each other better?"

He waited as the pause hung in the air. He'd tried to tell himself this impromptu evening was really about helping Violet. But if that's all it was, why wasn't he already in the car, driving there? Why was he standing in a classroom waiting for a sign from a red-headed romantic?

"Of course. We should probably get going."

Luke reached down to pick up the gym bag. He knew he should take the bag of grading as well, but he couldn't be responsible for his actions if he got close enough to take it from Amanda's hand. As he stood fully upright, he noticed the poster on the back wall declaring the start of The Cupid Caper.

Hearts, glitter, and a roly-poly guy in a diaper with a bow and arrow.

Clearly ol' Will Shakespeare knew the little winged man. No one would deny the English teacher did too. No one who knew line after line of poetry like she did could be charged with a lack of emotional insight.

So where did that leave him—the guy who wanted—no, needed—to make everything work according to logic and order?

Cupid stared at Luke from the confines of his poster. It had been so easy to deny all things relationships when he worked in the lab. The safety glasses and heavy lab coat reinforced every stereotype he'd believed about himself: scientific, analytical, reasoned, rational.

Luke thought that he was still that same guy, even though he'd traded the corporate lab for a public school's lab.

He wasn't used to being the subject, but clearly there was some experiment being played on him now by a short little golden-haired scientist in a diaper.

Luke shook his head and stepped forward out of the fog that had been holding him. It was time to quit being a variable and get back to being the control group.

Control. That was it. He just needed stay detached, approach this rationally and scientifically, and get back in control.

EVER SINCE THE WAITRESS brought their two glasses of iced tea, something had been different. Amanda wanted to squeeze the change in the air like the lemon wedge floating on top of her drink. She wanted to press Luke and find out just what had happened.

One minute she had to fight for breath in order to quote Shakespeare to him, and now, moments later, he was asking about the footwear she used as the drill team sponsor. She'd never transitioned from heart-racing to mundane quite so fast.

In fact, all she could think of as she stirred the lemon's juice into her tea, was that she'd wanted this moment for two years.

But now that she was at dinner with Luke Baker, well, she was bored out of her mind.

She wanted to notice Luke's dark blue eyes, or the generally strong set of his jaw. She wanted to focus on the cheap red glass candleholder that this Italian restaurant used to convey a little bit of atmosphere. She wanted to do anything but think about a line from Shakespeare's Richard II.

When words are scarce, they are seldom spent in vain.

Shakespeare was a liar.

Since they'd sat down, Luke's words had been few. And what conversation had been generated sounded ridiculous at best.

She just simply could not believe Luke Baker was the least bit interested in her description of why she liked split-soled jazz shoes when she held practices in the gym.

"That's really interesting, Amanda."

Oh, that was it. This had to end. "No it's not, Luke."

"What?" He looked at her with clear surprise.

"Tell me, what's your favorite brand of Bunsen burner."

"I've got the basic Humboldts in the classroom."

Amanda placed her glass of tea back on the table. "Fascinating."

"You don't really care, do you?" Luke rested his forearms on the table and leaned forward.

"Nope. And I doubt you care anything about split-soled jazz shoes." She leaned forward in her own imitation of his position. "What's going on, Luke?"

He sat back up straight. She'd gotten his attention. "What do you mean?"

"An hour ago, you were asking me for William Shakespeare's opinion on the scientific method, and now you're asking questions about which I know you have no true interest in the answer. Something happened, and I think you should be straight with me. You're the one who asked me to come tonight—you said you wanted to get to know me."

"I'm trying. I asked you about your work with the drill team. I assumed that was important to you."

"It is. I'm proud of my girls on the team. They work hard and I'm honored to be their director. But I just have a hard time believing you invited me to dinner tonight to talk about our plans for the spring competition circuit." Amanda picked up her napkin, folded it deliberately, then laid it back in her lap. She'd hoped he would take over during the pause in conversation, but he didn't. "So, cut to the chase."

She looked right at him, a small fountain of determination flowing into her mind and her spirit. All of a sudden, she needed the truth from him. She didn't think he knew about her secret crush, but she didn't want to know that the guy she'd watched from afar for so long suddenly thought better of inviting her out to a meal. Wouldn't that just confirm every thought she'd ever had that romance—except the kind in books—was dead?

Amanda flashed back to high school, when she'd been stood up for a dance after a football game. One simple careless act on the part of one stupid teenage boy made her second-guess herself for a long time. She really didn't want tonight to rank in the same general area.

And she really didn't want to go back to second-guessing herself. She'd stayed away from dating for a while because she was too busy.

But she knew she was lying to herself. The reality was that it felt far, far easier to watch anonymously from the sidelines than to engage and get pushed away, like she had every time before. She'd never even flirted with Luke Baker because she didn't want it to backfire on her.

And now today, when he'd actually made her want to pinch herself in that chemistry lab, it seemed like everything was rapidly coming to 'same song, different verse.'

"I don't know, Amanda. I owe you an apology. Just please don't reach for your keys. Not yet."

He must have been a mind reader. She'd already been thinking just that.

"Ok. Can we just start over then? Maybe talk about something we both care about? Like Violet Clark?"

Luke nodded and she noticed his broad shoulders drop a bit.

"I talked to the transportation department today," he said. "There definitely won't be any bus service for Violet to take advantage of. We're going to have to come up with a viable private transportation plan for her, or the STEM Academy won't be an option."

"Well, I might have an idea."

Luke leaned forward, resting his weight on his forearms again. "I'm open to any good ideas right now."

"Well, it has to do with The Cupid Caper."

"She can't ride a haiku to school, Amanda."

Amanda's mouth twitched up at the corners reflexively, paired with a short laugh. "I didn't mean like that, silly. The grand prize this year is a one-year lease on a car for the winners. I heard today that four different teachers got enrolled in The Cupid Caper. If we could find out who they are, and convince them to turn over their prize to Violet—if they win, of course—that would solve our problem right there."

"Sounds like an interesting idea, Amanda, but how do we make sure one of the teachers wins? We can't do that."

"Well, we know who two of the teachers are. Katelyn Pantego is another one. And we know that the winners are determined by popular vote on the night of the dance, based on the couples who accurately guess each other's secret Cupids during the week."

"Pantego's out." Luke picked up the knife from his place setting and drummed the edge on the table. "I went to talk to Liz Langton today like I said I would. She said Katelyn was embarrassed by it and didn't want to take part. But she wouldn't give any other details. She just said we didn't need to worry, that the nominations didn't come from a student."

Amanda threw out her hands. "Because they came from her!"

As she gestured, the side of her palm came into full contact with her iced tea glass, sending it rolling on its side and draining into a big puddle on the floor. At once, six tables' worth of eyes turned and stared right at her.

Great, Amanda thought. *Red hair. Red shirt. Red cheeks.*

"I just told her about the tiramisu here." Luke spoke up loudly enough for everyone to hear. "It's worthy of such a reaction. You should try it."

He held out his napkin. Amanda took it gratefully. While most of the tea had landed on the floor, some of it had also landed square in her lap, soaking through her napkin. She pushed hers aside and tried to blot some of the liquid out of her pants as best she could.

"You ok?" Luke's low voice came across as measured, edged with concern.

"I'll be fine. But now I'm going to need tiramisu."

"We can arrange that." He smiled confidently. "But first, we've got to get back to the subject at hand. What do you mean The Cupid Caper entries came from her?"

Amanda felt her adrenaline cranking again. The whole thing just seemed so fishy. But she didn't have any reason to doubt Lindsay, who'd always been a trustworthy student and drill team officer. "One of my drill team officers is also an officer in Student Council. She said she handled the teacher envelopes and the forms had all been filled out in Liz's handwriting."

Luke's brow furrowed, teasing a set of wrinkles across his strong forehead. "So one of your officers put together our envelopes and the other two. Did she say who they were?"

"You know...I didn't even think to ask." Amanda could have slapped herself upside the head. "I was too shocked when she said the forms were signed off by Liz. My mind started swirling."

She looked straight at Luke. His eyes were steady and focused intently back on her.

And darn it if her mind didn't start swirling again.

Amanda started talking again as fast as she could to keep her mind from running off the rails. "Well, we know Pantego is one of the others. So that just leaves one other person. But honestly, I don't see how that helps us with the Violet issue, anyway."

"I don't think it matters." Luke's voice sounded assured.

"You have an idea?"

"I do." He took a sip of tea, then tapped the table for emphasis as he began to speak. "You just said the winners of The Cupid Caper are ultimately determined by popular vote, right?"

Amanda nodded. "It's high school. Everything is ultimately determined by popular vote."

Luke shrugged. "Then it's simple."

"What's simple?"

"Winning."

"You sound like Charlie Sheen."

Luke threw an exaggerated scowl across the table. "No. I'm not crazy, and there's no tiger blood in my tea. We just have to be the most popular couple in the school. If we can convince the kids to vote for us instead of one of their own, we can sign over that car lease to Violet. It's the perfect plan."

It wasn't a bad plan. Except for one minor detail. "But what about the other teacher who was signed up for The Cupid Caper?"

"What about them? Now that Pantego's out, they don't stand a chance."

"Yeah, but what if we're not matched together? What if you were matched to Katelyn and I was matched to the other guy?"

A slow grin cracked Luke's face. She could see each tooth clearly in the glow from the cheap candle.

"Doesn't matter. We have three days. By the time that dance rolls around Saturday night, no one at Port Provident High will be able to think of any other Cupid contestant."

Amanda's pulse began to bounce like a bumble bee going from one pollen-filled flower to the next. She'd been carrying around a secret crush on Luke for so long that she had to pinch herself that Luke's plan was all an act, a carefully choreographed three days designed to ultimately help a student. When the weekend came, Amanda would go back to teaching the world's greatest love stories—without actually living one herself—and Luke would go back to packing his boxes for the STEM Academy.

Unless...

"'All the world's a stage, and all the men and women merely players," Amanda quoted as a thought occurred to her. "'They have their exits and their entrances, and one man in his time plays many parts.'"

"Your boy Will S. again, right?" Luke picked up on the time-worn verse.

"Yes, the monologue from the melancholy Jaques in *As You Like It*."

"What do you like?" Will settled his strong chin into the palm of his hand and looked at her with a gaze she couldn't quite place. It made a tingle stronger than February's crisp wind dance down her spine. She liked the way the tingle made her feel aware and alive.

She could imagine why Shakespeare or one of the other great poets wanted to capture this essence in words, to remember it always.

"I like your idea. Helping Violet like that, I mean." She liked the tingle too, but she didn't want to let on about that.

Luke didn't move. "What about me?"

"What do you mean what about you?" The spark and crackle effervescing its way through her veins started to pop like so many oversized bubbles.

"Me. Do you like me?"

The popping reached her cheeks and started to heat them with a blush. "Well, um, sure. But I mean, I don't really know you."

Ineloquent answers like this were why Amanda knew she'd never have a poetry-worthy romance. There would be no love like a red, red rose. No comparing to a summer's day. No how do I love thee, let me count the ways.

It was so much easier for her to teach the classic stories of love. Because goodness knew no Romeo would risk a run-in with Capulet kin for an answer like the one she just gave Luke.

"You're going to have to do better than that. Take two. Do you like me?"

Now the fizz and crackle began to give way to a slippery nervous sensation at the base curve of her stomach. She couldn't even think of a witty retort taken from one of the masters of literature. She would have to have to answer this on her own.

But she was completely put on the spot. How could Amanda answer honestly without blurting out that she'd had a crush on Luke for two years?'

"You sat in front of me at your first staff meeting. I don't think I paid attention to any of the presentations."

Amanda felt a strange combination of mortification and freedom. She felt completely embarrassed to expose herself like that to Luke. But at the same time, relief flowed from not having to keep her secret to herself.

She held her breath for a moment, waiting at the conversational fork in the road. She needed to know Luke's reaction so she could know if she would have to feel awkward around him, now that he knew her secret or not.

"Much better. That's a good story. I'm pretty impressed that you made that up on the fly." Luke leaned back in his chair. "I think that will be very convincing."

Wait. Convincing?

Luke continued. "So go with that, starting tomorrow. We'll be so over the top that everyone will have to vote for us."

At that moment, the waiter brought their dinner. They continued to make small talk and plans for the next few days. Luke had some good ideas and Amanda found herself laughing at some of the scenarios he wanted to carry out. Some she talked him out of. Others, she added her own two cents on.

But as she listened to the object of her multi-year crush talk about acting in love for the remainder of the week, Amanda began to wonder if maybe it didn't have to be an act.

Maybe she could use the cover of The Cupid Caper to overcome her inhibitions and show Luke how she'd really felt the last two years.

And maybe, just maybe, when it was all over, he'd want to keep playing the part...this time for real.

She'd need to swallow her pride and her recent protests, and enlist the best actress she knew, one time Broadway understudy and the queen of the Port Provident High School stage, Lisa Fleming.

Lisa would help her best friend out—heck she practically begged Amanda to send a note to Luke for The Cupid Caper. She'd be smug, in that way only Lisa could be, but she'd also turn cartwheels to help her friend. Like all thespians, Lisa had a big heart and an even bigger penchant for making the moment count.

The waiter sat a square of tiramisu, dusted with a spray of cocoa powder, in front of Amanda.

"Where did that come from?"

Luke speared his own slice almost as soon as it materialized in front of him. "I told you—ok, I told everyone—that it was great. I took the liberty of ordering you a slice while you were in the restroom earlier. Consider it my first gift to my new girlfriend."

Just for a moment, Amanda shoved aside the knowledge that to Luke, this was all an act. A means to an end.

She savored the idea of an unexpected romantic gesture from a suitor, like Romeo calling under Juliet's window. This was how it happened in all the best love stories.

"In that case, thank you, my dear." She smiled sweetly back at Luke, thinking of the phone call she was about to make to Lisa to get started on a Cupid-inspired plan of her own. It made her a little nervous. She'd never been this bold before.

But she had one big chance. She needed to take it.

She needed to write her own story.

If all the world was a stage, well, Amanda Marsh decided to make her debut in the spotlight.

Chapter Four

"OH MY GOODNESS, YOU scared me."

The lights in Amanda's room were on, but Luke couldn't see where the voice was coming from. "Lisa, is that you?"

"Yeah. Luke?"

He saw a figure stand up from behind the desk.

"Correct."

"Oh my gosh, what on earth is that?" Lisa's shriek broke the pre-bell silence. The school wouldn't actually open to students for another fifteen minutes. But anyone within a ten mile radius probably just heard Lisa.

"Cupig. What's it look like?" Luke stuck his head out from behind the life-sized stuffed pig, complete with wings, diaper, and glittery gold bow and arrow. "I think he's going to look great at the desk."

"Cupig. Oh my goodness gracious." Lisa patted the angelic porker on his hamburger-sized nose. "But why?"

"The Cupid Caper. Haven't you heard? Amanda's my Cupid Crush."

Lisa nodded her head. "I heard something about that."

May as well start the campaign now. Every person he convinced of his true love for Amanda could help convince someone else. And then that vote for Violet's car would be in the bag.

"The Cupid Caper really came at the perfect time. You know, I'm leaving soon for the STEM Academy. But now I can do something special for Amanda before I go."

Lisa stood back against the wall, holding something behind her. "Really?"

"You don't think Cupig is too much, do you?" He carried the pig back to its new place of honor in Amanda's chair, then scooted Cupig up to the desk.

Lisa dropped the bag she'd been holding on the floor, then gave it a quick kick under the table. It was just a simple plastic bag from a grocery store, but she'd tied the handles together like bunny ears and Luke couldn't get any idea of what was inside.

"Well, it certainly seems you've gone...um...whole hog."

"Isn't that what you're supposed to do? I mean, she teaches poetry and love stories. Wouldn't she love to be swept off her feet?"

Lisa's oversized silver loop earrings bounced as she nodded enthusiastically. "Yes, yes she would."

Luke had an idea. Maybe he didn't need to just convince Lisa. She was one of the most popular teachers in the school—everyone loved the feisty drama teacher. If he got her on his side, that would definitely be worth votes. "So, you two are friends. What else should I do?"

"Well, I'm not sure how you top that." Lisa pointed squarely at the porcine Valentine watching their every move. "But she's definitely a girly girl. Hearts, flowers, all that jazz. She loves love."

"She's not dating anyone, right?" It had just occurred to Luke that he probably ought to find this one out. Granted, he figured she would have mentioned it last night when he started scheming. But the last thing Luke needed was an angry boyfriend challenging Cupig—or him—to a fight behind the bleachers.

"No, she's not." Lisa looked at Cupig, then turned her eyes on Luke with a flash of fire. "I meant what I said. She's in love with love. She doesn't date much because she has high expectations, and I don't mean that in a bad way. She wants someone who makes her feel special. And I want someone who won't take advantage of a woman with a very sweet heart who would do anything for someone she cares about—whether that's a student, a friend, or someone who could mean something more."

Luke started to respond, but Lisa held up both of her hands, stopping him before he even got out a syllable.

"The Cupid Caper may be geared toward high school students. But my best friend's heart isn't child's play. I expect you to treat her right."

Lisa's ultimatum made Luke want to clear the air and explain that it was all an act, a carefully-scripted few days designed to benefit a student both he and Amanda admired. He knew he wasn't going to hurt Amanda—she was in on it. He didn't want Lisa worrying about her best friend, either.

But he knew the best way to win the contest was to have Lisa fully bought in. He needed her to believe that this particular Cupid Caper was real.

"Of course I will." He could at least answer that honestly. He wouldn't do anything to hurt Amanda. He'd gotten to know her more in the last two days than he had in the last two years. He liked her copper hair, her concern for her students, and how she always seemed to have the perfect literary quote up her sleeve.

The Cupid Caper would just be temporary, but he knew his newfound admiration of the English teacher would stay with him.

"Good. As long as you're more Cupig than stereotypic pig, I think we'll be fine." Lisa walked across the room, heading toward the door as she spoke. "You know, she's a great girl with a big heart. She deserves the best. No games."

After Lisa left, Luke stood alone in the center of Amanda's class for a moment. The walls were covered with educational posters bearing the portraits of the world's greatest writers, projects created by her students, and one giant sign for The Cupid Caper.

Luke thought for a minute about what Lisa said on her way out the door.

She's a great girl with a big heart.

Anyone who walked in this classroom could see that clearly. Amanda Marsh loved literature, loved her students.

As someone who loved the subject he taught and the students he taught it to, he suddenly felt a pull of connection to Amanda he hadn't previously noticed before. The last time he'd been in this classroom with her, he'd felt an undeniable physical attraction to her.

Now, though, he seemed to notice a bit more.

No games.

He remembered flicking that envelope of poetry in his trash can yesterday with a feeling of smug superiority. He thought he was far too analytical for something as silly as The Cupid Caper. But then he'd found a reason to play along.

Luke stared at the oversized pink rectangle on the wall with the badly-drawn picture of Cupid adorning the top left corner. He didn't want to play games.

He wanted to win.

Not a car.

He wanted to win Amanda Marsh's heart.

EVER SINCE SHE'D WALKED in the door to see a giant stuffed animal named Cupig seated behind her desk, Amanda had walked around with a smile on her face. She didn't remember a time when she'd ever felt this upbeat about a relationship.

Or an un-relationship.

She knew where Luke stood. He had a plan and a goal. She supported the goal. It was noble. It would change Violet's life to have the tools necessary to go to the STEM Academy. Amanda had finished reviewing Violet's essay during her planning period today. It was exactly as she expected: smart, well-written, and an overall polished effort. Between her strong grades, Luke's mentorship on the application, and the short feature on what being an inaugural student at the STEM Academy would mean to her, Amanda felt confidently assured that Violet would earn a place at the Academy.

And so that just left the question of transportation. Luke seemed certain that they could win the big prize at Saturday night's dance.

Which meant Amanda would continue to play along. Luke would never know her actions were the real deal.

She thought about Cupig and how pleasant it had been to start the morning with the gift of his smiling pink face. She'd always wanted surprises and romance in a relationship.

But now she wanted one more thing.

Certainty.

The certainty that Luke would still be there after Saturday. Luke had his plan. She had hers.

And so, after the final bell had rung for the day, Amanda made it a priority to take the back stairs up to the science hallway and head for Luke's lab.

Luke faced his computer and didn't notice Amanda as she walked in the door.

Time to be bold, Amanda. It starts now.

If Luke wanted over-the-top Cupid-worthy affection, he was going to get it.

She summoned her inner Juliet, filled up with enough courage to tell off an entire hall of Capulets.

And then she ran.

Partly because it seemed like what Juliet would do if she saw Romeo after a long day.

But mostly because the quicker she committed to the course of action, the less time she had to talk herself out of it.

"What the..."

Luke spun around in his chair as Amanda wrapped her arms around his chest once her feet carried her close enough. The sudden turn of the stool-height chair knocked Amanda's balance off kilter and her right ankle got twisted behind her left.

She felt the fall begin, a type of slow motion that left her entirely cognizant of the details. She could see her mortification coming like a locomotive about to plow into an object on the tracks.

What she couldn't see, until it was too late to do anything but try to fling herself out of the way, was that by not releasing her arms instantly, she was taking Luke down with her.

The chair tumbled and the metal frame hit the cheap linoleum floor with a loud crash. Amanda rolled one way and Luke landed on his bicep and rolled the other. Amanda pushed herself up on her right arm and looked around. As Luke raised himself, she smiled.

"Um...hi?"

He scratched the side of his head, just over his ear. She'd never noticed what a precise haircut he had before. The dark edge of the hair curved perfectly and evenly over the ear, then trailed to a spot about one-third of the way down his neck, where it stopped with a clean, sharp edge and raced across the skin in a ruler-straight line.

She'd never noticed it before, but she wasn't surprised that even Luke's haircut would be organized and orderly. Just like everything else in his life.

Amanda began to second-guess herself. Maybe she had the wrong idea. Maybe she was a spastic square peg trying to force herself into the round hole of Luke's life.

She thought of the opening lines of O'Shaughnessy's Ode: "We are the music makers/And we are the dreamers of dreams." Aside from the fact that she had no musical ability, she'd always felt a kinship to those lines. No one would ever deny she was a dreamer of dreams.

As they both sat on the floor, downed chair between them, Amanda took a hard look at Luke. She saw the short, even-edged hair, the dark blue eyes beneath a straight brow with a touch of heaviness, the chiseled lines of his jaw and a well-muscled torso that could only be attributed to hours of work in a gym, not luck.

She choreographed dances, expression set to music. Luke choreographed his entire life, down to how he was going to win a high school contest.

"Hi." He looked at her a little sheepishly, as though he was still trying to figure out exactly what had just happened. "You wanted to talk to me?"

"I wanted to thank you for Cupig. He's adorable." Amanda stood up and brushed her hands down the front of her lightweight wool pants to smooth them.

"You're welcome." Luke's wariness transformed into a warm smile as he stood, and picked the chair up. "I saw it in a window on my way home last night. I figured we had the rest of the week. May as well start with a bang. Go big or go home, right? Of course, some of the fun is missing because you and I already know who we're matched with, so there's no trying to solve the secret of who is leaving the gifts."

"Well, maybe not, but he was still definitely a surprise."

Amanda wished her own plan to surprise him hadn't gone completely awry. She remembered her breath stopping just a little yesterday when his hand touched her arm as he picked up her gym bag. She didn't know exactly what she'd been hoping for with that over-the-top hug, but another moment like that would have been something she could have saved as a memory in case her twist on Luke's plan for The Cupid Caper fell as spectacularly as that chair just now.

"Good. I'm glad you liked him. Are you about to head out for the day?"

"No drill team practice today and I'm strangely caught up on my grading. I think I'm going to leave at a respectable hour for a change."

"Well, then, let me shut down here and I'll walk you out to your car." He punched a few buttons on his computer. "Hopefully there will still be enough people around to notice us together. That would be good, wouldn't it?"

Amanda nodded. She leaned back against the high table behind her and looked up at the clock on the wall.

She felt a delicate pricking across the top of her right foot and looked down.

"Mouse! Mouse!"

A small, white rodent with a pale pink tail scampered off the edge of her black shoe and toward the corner of the knee space under Luke's desk.

Without thinking, Amanda reacted, jumping to the side.

Luke spun around to check out her shriek and Amanda bounced into his chest with the side of her body.

Instinctively, she wrapped her arms around his shoulder and tried to pick her right foot up off the floor. Under her trembling palms, he felt like a solid brick standing between her and the offensive bundle of fur, ears, and tail.

"I think you found Kevin." Luke didn't move.

The crown of Amanda's head rested below Luke's chin and the exhale after his words gently stirred the top of her hair. Her heart raced like a finely-tuned race car competing for a title.

But she couldn't tell if it was all because of the mouse.

She leaned in a little more closely, felt the piqued cotton of his collared casual shirt against the bare skin of her arms below the short cotton sleeves of her own shirt.

Amanda knew this surge in her veins wasn't all due to the mouse.

"Kevin?"

"White mouse, about so long?" Luke spread his thumb and forefinger about two and a half inches apart and moved his hand closer to Amanda's face. With his other hand, he held her steady.

She fought the paradox of wanting to run far, far away from the mouse, but never wanting to leave the closeness of Luke. "Mmm-hmm."

Amanda realized she'd been reduced to speaking in monosyllabic muffles. She knew it meant something significant, but couldn't really process any coherent thoughts.

And again, if she was being honest, it had nothing to do with the mouse.

"That's Kevin. He escaped from the biology lab next door yesterday. Kathy Moore's been looking for him. He's the control for a feeding experiment they're doing. I expect he got jealous that Mortimer gets dessert every night."

As the shock of the mouse-moment passed, Amanda slowly pulled her hand off Luke's shoulder. She could feel the definitions of the muscle groups as her fingertips slid toward his chest.

Luke turned his head and looked right in Amanda's eyes. She couldn't tell much difference between the black of his pupils and the intense blue of the irises.

"Maybe you shouldn't do that, Amanda." His voice sounded lower and more measured than usual.

Amanda's mind formed a single coherent thought about her one wish, to make Luke think of The Cupid Caper as more than a joke. To make him think of her as more than just someone who worked at the same school. To make the dream she'd held for two years a reality.

She willed herself to not back down.

"Do what?"

He flicked a hand at the base of her neck and moved the heavy curtain of curls.

"That."

Apparently the monosyllabic disease had gotten to both of them. She took a breath, hoping it would steady her. It didn't. Instead, the intake of air heightened every sense she had. The undernotes of Luke's sandalwood cologne stood out like the clean woodsiness of the outdoors after a rain. His pupils dilated slightly, deepening the darkness. The dryness at the front of her mouth pushed back across the curve of her tongue. Her palms warmed as they molded to the plane of his chest.

And the sound of two teenage girls talking in the hallway sounded so loud, Amanda almost thought they were headed for the chemistry lab.

"Hey, Dr. B!" A high-pitched voice shouted in a sing-song manner. "Aaaand Miss M. What's going on?"

Amanda pulled her gaze down from Luke's eyes and looked over his shoulder. Lindsay Moore had stopped suddenly in the doorway.

"Mouse," Amanda said succinctly.

Luke pulled back but didn't turn around to face the girls. The muscle at the back of his jaw flexed twice before he spoke. "Mouse."

"I was just dropping off your voting sheet for The Cupid Caper. You'll need to fill this out tomorrow and drop it off in the box in the cafeteria." She leaned forward and laid the bright pink paper carefully on the desk closest to the door. "But maybe you've already made your guess."

The young blonde ducked her head and turned quickly back toward the hallway, her friend in an equal hurry to get out of the chemistry lab.

"I'm going to return Kevin next door." Luke walked away from Amanda and bent over the corner where the mouse had backed himself into. "Are you still heading home?"

"Yeah. I think I'm going to go get my things from my room." She decided to play one more card, to keep being bold. Her breath caught in her throat a little as she forced the words out. "Are you still walking me to my car?"

He cupped the frightened mouse in his two hands. She remembered their gentle touch on her only moments before.

"I can. But I'm pretty sure that once those two girls start talking, we're not going to have to convince anyone of anything else between now and Saturday night."

"I NEED COFFEE." ACTUALLY, Luke knew needed something stronger, but it was only three-thirty in the afternoon.

He couldn't think straight anymore. It had been at least fifteen minutes, and he could swear he still felt the touch of Amanda's hand on his chest. The phantom press of her five fingertips lingered.

"What about MugBugs? It's just right over there." Amanda pointed at the corner of the strip center across the street from the high school.

Ironically, a tall, steaming cup of coffee as black as the night was the only thing he could think of to cool him off.

He'd thought it this morning after talking to Lisa.

Now he knew it for sure.

This wasn't a game he was playing with Amanda.

This was for real. But how was he supposed to let her know? He knew everything he felt and did from the moment she jumped into his arms was pure, driven instinct.

He knew hers was too. But Luke felt pretty certain her instinct had been driven by a rodent-induced near-fainting spell.

For once, he wished he wasn't the analytical, lab rat—pardon the pun—chemistry guy. He wished he could have been a literary wonk like Amanda and pulled the perfect verse out of his brain. He'd have given anything to let Shakespeare or Wordsworth do the talking at a moment like this.

"Luke? You're really quiet."

At least she couldn't read his thoughts. They careened off the synapses in his brain loud and clear.

"Sorry. Just thinking. MugBugs sounds fine." He looked at her, poised to unlock her compact sedan. He didn't want her to find out what he was thinking before he had a chance to organize his thoughts and present them in the right way. But he didn't want this to be the end, either. He didn't want to go back home tonight and sit around and think about Amanda.

He wanted to be around Amanda. "You want to come with me?"

A thoughtful look clouded her eyes briefly. "Ok. Let me just lock my bag up in the trunk."

Once she'd secured all her belongings, they set off toward the crosswalk. As they waited for the light to change, Luke's fingers itched to reach out and close the distance between his hand and hers.

He straightened his pointer finger and teased against the side of hers.

She opened a space between it and her middle finger. Given the subtle go-ahead, Luke laced his fingers between hers, and as the little symbol in the crosswalk light changed from orange to white, he took a step and guided her across the street, trying to stay focused on the intersection of the streets and not the intersection of their hands.

"Is the line out the door?"

The coffee shop looked packed with students. After being caught by Lindsay earlier, Luke didn't feel quite up for a repeat.

"Well, that's no good." Luke wasn't sure if he felt greater disappointment about not getting coffee or not getting to hold Amanda's hand much longer.

Amanda paused on the sidewalk once they were back across the street. "I don't live that far from here and I have a coffee pot. It's nothing fancy, but I can at least guarantee there won't be any students lining up at my door."

"Amanda, I really don't want to inconvenience you."

Truthfully, he knew the only reason things hadn't moved to the next step in the chemistry lab was because of the arrival of the students on the scene. He couldn't make a move like that without having his plan fully thought through. He couldn't scare Amanda off.

"You're not inconveniencing me. After all, you brought me a giant Cupig. Coffee kind of seems like the least I could do."

He watched her red hair blow back in the strong February breeze and remembered his earlier thought to himself. He didn't want to go home to think about Amanda. He wanted to be with her.

Against his better judgment, he replied affirmatively. "Ok, that sounds good."

They walked back to their cars in the faculty parking lot and Amanda told Luke the directions to her townhouse, only a few minutes away. As he drove the handful of miles, he kept thinking about the last two days.

He'd never almost lost control like he'd now done twice with Amanda.

How had he gone two years without noticing her?

Luke walked up to the door and rang the bell. The only answer was scientific. Sometimes, people saw—or didn't see—what they wanted to see. That's why there were time-tested steps in the Scientific Method.

You posed a question, did your research, formulated a hypothesis, and then conducted an experiment to test that hypothesis.

This was no different than what he'd teach his students. He'd never noticed Amanda Marsh because he'd never posed the question. He'd never been looking. He'd been waiting for everything in this new phase of his life to line up before he jumped back into dating again.

Somewhere along the line, he'd forgotten the thrill of adrenaline.

At some point during the years, he'd disregarded the rush of discovery.

The door opened and Amanda's smile greeted him.

For the first time in a long time, he formed a hypothesis. Luke hypothesized that he'd kiss Amanda Marsh before he walked back out this door.

It was time to conduct the most important experiment he'd ever done. It was time to test for mutual chemistry between him and one fiery English teacher who wouldn't leave his mind.

"If you want to make yourself comfortable, I'll go ahead and get the coffee started." Amanda gestured toward the sofa in her living room. "The remote is on the table if you want to turn on the TV."

Luke didn't think the sound of afternoon programming would really add to his experiment. "Does your TV have any of those music channels?"

"I think so." Amanda spoke over the rattle of coffee mugs and the rush of water flowing from the sink into the coffee pot. "They're at the very end. Like nine-hundred-and-something."

Luke began to flip around until he found the right channel. Soft contemporary music began to play. He adjusted the volume until it filled the air as gentle background noise.

"You've got a nice place, Amanda." The room had been decorated in cool blues and silvers. "For some reason, I was expecting tufted sofas and antiques."

She came into the living room bearing both a smile and a mug of coffee in each hand. "Just because I teach about literature that's been around for centuries doesn't mean I want to live with furniture that also has."

"Fair enough. I guess it would have been a bit much to see your living room arranged like the Globe Theatre too." He looked around at the pictures hanging on the walls in groups all around the living room. Each had been rimmed in a wide white mat, and framed with a simple black frame. "But wait, what's that?"

Luke pointed at a group near the back window.

"Um, well...that's the Globe Theatre." Amanda smiled broadly. She knew she'd been caught. "That's from two summers ago. I took a group of students for two weeks. We went all over England, soaking up the history and the culture."

"You know, I've been a lot of places, but I've never been to London. I usually go someplace with nature involved—mountain climbing, safaris, diving. Or I jump from perfectly good bridges and buildings and planes. Things like that. Tell me about London."

Amanda's whole face took on a soft glow. It could have been the steam coming off the coffee mug she clutched tightly in her hands, but Luke knew it wasn't.

"It's just an amazing juxtaposition of the old and the new. On one hand, you have all the history—The Tower, Parliament, Buckingham Palace, The Victoria and Albert Museum, even Churchill's War Rooms. But then, it's a thoroughly modern city. The London Eye is this giant ferris wheel with pods you stand in. It dominates the skyline along the Thames now. But yet, it belongs there as much as the rest of it does. I guess that's what I love about literature too. The best of it has stood the test of time and it becomes a shared experience."

Luke thought back to the experience they'd shared earlier in the day. "I'd never really thought of it like that. You know the 'O Captain, My Captain' scene in the movie *Dead Poets' Society*?"

"One of my favorites."

"I figured as much. I always thought it was a little cheesy. But maybe you're right. Maybe the lines and books we've known all our lives give us common bonds. Who's your favorite writer?"

Amanda sat her mug down on the low black coffee table in front of her. "Well, I doubt this comes as a surprise to you, but probably Shakespeare."

Luke shook his head. "No, not surprising at all. But why?"

"Well, for one, everyone knows at least some Shakespeare. Just about everyone you encounter has heard of *Romeo and Juliet*, at least." She gestured with her hands as she spoke, pulling Luke into her explanation as thoroughly as if she were touching him and guiding him. "'But soft, what light through yonder window breaks? It is the east, and Juliet is the sun. Arise, fair sun, and kill the envious moon, who is already sick and pale with grief...'"

Luke jumped into the pause. "You want to go on and recite the whole thing, don't you?"

Amanda smiled wistfully. "I could. But I won't."

"Why not?"

"Because no one really wants to listen to an English teacher prattle on about Shakespeare." She looked right at Luke and the effect was like a compass zoned in on true north. "Not when they're eighteen. And not when they're older."

If his English teacher had recited the classics with half the intensity that flowed with Amanda's words, he might have found himself with an entirely different appreciation for literature. Most of his life, he'd dismissed novels and poetry as just nonsense written by dreamers.

But sitting in front of him was a real, live dreamer. And nothing about her was nonsense.

Luke came around the side of the living room, as though he wanted to see the rest of Amanda's pictures. Truthfully, though, he only had eyes for Amanda. It only took a handful of steps to close the gap between them.

"So tell me," he said, standing so close to her that he could note the gentle rise and fall of her chest as she breathed.

"Yes?" Her voice was quiet, like the rustle of an angel's wings.

"Tell me what Juliet said back to Romeo."

The rhythm of her chest sped up slightly. "She replied with some of the most famous words ever written. 'O Romeo, Romeo! Wherefore art thou Romeo?'"

"Ah yes, I've heard that one." Luke reached out and brushed a lock of hair behind Amanda's ear. "She was up in a tower, right?"

Amanda's reply was bracketed by a sharp intake of breath. "Not a tower. Her balcony."

"And Romeo was below, right?"

Amanda nodded, the movement of her head barely noticeable.

Luke trailed two fingers through Amanda's hair, and swept them down the curve of her jaw, then let them come to rest at the center of her chin.

With his free arm, he circled her shoulders, then let his hand slide down the groove of her spine. With every knot of vertebrae he passed, Amanda's rhythmic breathing became less regular and more jagged.

Luke's breathing began to imitate Amanda's. He could feel the surge of adrenaline in his veins, and the need to make happen what was coming.

But he held back, wanting to make the moment last. Wanting to make it something Amanda would remember. Wanting to make it not about a stunt at a high school dance, but an emotion they could build on.

He'd vowed that he'd make Amanda see he was about more than The Cupid Caper. He knew she'd agreed to pretend like they were head-over-heels to help Violet. But somewhere along the line, it turned into more than that for him.

Luke couldn't tell Amanda he wasn't pretending—not until after the dance. He didn't want to scare her off. Violet needed their crazy plan to work, and he didn't want to jeopardize that.

So he needed this moment to be true. He needed to tell Amanda that Cupid had struck for real. Without using words.

Luke flattened his hand at the base of Amanda's spine and pressed the two fingers under her chin with a gentle force.

As her chin tilted up, her lips parted slightly. The simple instinctive move drove him to the point of insistence. He closed his eyes and lowered his head.

The instant his lips joined hers, all the words Amanda had quoted earlier filled his mind. He felt the fire of the sun, the glow of the moon, and the emotional drive of two young lovers plotting on a star-lit balcony.

Luke brushed his hand down her neck and curved it behind, deepening the kiss. Amanda didn't pull back and Luke knew this was one of those times when all the science and logic in the world couldn't quantify what had happened in this room.

Slowly, he pulled back. He wanted to see her eyes. Wanted to know if she'd felt the same electric force that had danced between them. He took a small step away, clearing some space between them, but he didn't move the hand across her lower back. His palm still fit to her lumbar like a glove with a heat that he could feel deep inside.

Amanda's eyes were wide. For the first time since he'd really started paying attention, he didn't see even a fleck of gray in them. They shone as green as a light at an intersection, stuck in the 'go' position.

Luke felt a kinship with that light. He wanted to go for more, to taste the warm tingle of coffee on her lips again.

They stood there for a moment, neither saying anything. The silence made Luke nervous.

"Did I make the coffee too strong?" Amanda finally said.

Luke released his hand and brought it back to his side. The solar-like spark he'd been feeling just extinguished. Of all the reactions he could have envisioned, having Amanda just laugh off that kiss hadn't made his short list.

"Now you know why I can't go in a Starbucks. Can't keep my hands off the baristas." Luke decided to just play along.

Only seconds ago, he'd wanted to convey to her exactly how he felt. Now all he could do was hope Amanda thought it had been a caffeine-induced joke.

As ridiculous as that was, it beat the alternative.

It beat knowing that he'd finally let his guard down to someone who was just biding her time until Saturday night, when Cupid would go off-duty.

Chapter Five

AMANDA STOPPED BY LUKE'S classroom after a hectic Thursday to deliver her day's present for The Cupid Caper, only to find a gray-haired lady sitting behind the tall desk at the front of the lab.

"He has a meeting today at the Administration Building about the STEM Academy. I've been here since lunch. You can just leave that up here and he'll get it tomorrow."

The substitute teacher took the paper hand of the giant balloon in the shape of lips, complete with arms and legs. She guided it to a corner by the computer and pushed it to the back.

Amanda couldn't quite put her finger on it, but watching the woman wrinkle her nose at the oversized gift made her feel self-conscious. Since last night, Amanda had been running all sorts of scenarios in her head.

She'd bought this crazy balloon to show that she wasn't taking yesterday's kiss too seriously.

Amanda knew the whole thing was part of an act—so she figured she'd just poke fun at what happened. That way, Luke would never know how his hand on her waist kept her from falling to the ground because she'd gone weak in the knees the moment his fingers brushed through her hair.

If she brought a pair of giant walking balloon lips into his classroom, she hoped he'd never find out that the only thing she'd thought of for hours was the feel of his mouth as it pressed to hers. And if she acted like all she cared about was winning the grand prize in The Cupid Caper, he'd never find out her little secret—that the only love story she wanted to hear about was her own with him.

Except that there was no love story between them.

There was no chance to make light of what had happened.

And there was no Luke to brighten her day just by looking at him.

"Are you sure you should be leaving that in here?" The older woman looked back at the balloon, gently swaying like a dancer as the draft from the air conditioner hit it. "Seems kind of inappropriate for a teacher to be bringing a big kiss to another teacher. Times have changed since I had my own classroom, I guess."

Amanda nodded briefly and mumbled something about The Cupid Caper, and how it raised money for students. She turned and left the room without a backward glance.

She returned to her classroom to find Cupig staring right at her, and she felt her heart break a little at the site of the oversized Valentine.

"I wish you were for real, Cupig," Amanda said flatly.

"You wish the stuffed pig was real?" Lisa stuck her head in the doorway, purse in hand. "That would be interesting. A giant, live pig wearing a diaper. Would probably generate just as much intrigue as what actually goes into the sauce on spaghetti day down in the cafeteria."

Amanda turned away from Cupig and tried not to blush at getting caught talking to a stuffed animal. At least it was just one of her best friends. She'd still have to do some explaining, but not quite as much.

"No, I don't wish he was a real pig. Just that the sentiment behind him was."

"What do you mean?" Lisa leaned against the door frame.

"I know that Luke and I agreed to go big or go home on this whole thing with The Cupid Caper. I'll let you in on a secret. Once we found ourselves involved, I took your advice and we committed to doing what it takes to win that car lease and turn it over to Violet." Amanda sat on the top of one of the student desks. "But it's hard."

"It's hard pretending to be Luke's Not-So-Secret Cupid?"

"No, it's hard pretending that's all it is to me." Amanda threw her hands up in the air, then slapped them down on her legs. "Do you know how hard it is to get kissed by the guy you've had a crush on for years—and to know that it doesn't mean a darned thing to him?"

Lisa popped off the doorway. "Wait. He kissed you?"

"Last night." There was no use trying to deny it to Lisa. She'd just sniff it out in mere seconds, exactly like a bloodhound.

"Where?" Lisa's eyes narrowed as she began to ferret out details.

"At my place."

"He was at your house?"

"He wanted coffee. MugBugs was packed, so I said I could make us some." Amanda's mind thought back to the look on

Luke's face when she brought him the coffee as he checked out her photos on the wall.

Lisa nodded deliberately. "Mmm-hmm. And then he made dessert?"

"Lisa. Really."

Her dark blonde curls shook. "Look, I'm just calling it like I see it."

"Well, stop, because you're not helping things one bit." Amanda began to feel even more uneasy than she had felt only moments before under the steel gaze of the substitute teacher.

"You want my help?"

Amanda didn't quite know how to respond. "I think I'm beyond help, Lisa."

"Come on, let's go." She lifted the hand that carried her smaller bag and waved it in Amanda's direction. "We've got work to do."

Amanda slid down from where she'd been sitting. "What are you talking about?"

"The Cupid Caper. You need a dress. Maybe you're right. Maybe he *is* just in it for the outcome of tomorrow night's drawing. But it's up to you to make him think about something other than a car lease. You need to knock him dead tomorrow night. And if there's one thing I know about, it's costumes. We are going to get you a dress that's going to knock his socks off. Grab your stuff and let's go."

Amanda wanted to protest. She wanted to argue that it wouldn't matter.

But it had been a long day. And a little bit of retail therapy sounded nice.

Even if it sounded completely futile.

LUKE STOPPED BY THE school on his way home to pick up some materials he'd wanted to read over again before tomorrow's lesson. The last bell for the day had rung hours ago, and only a handful of students remained on the campus.

He took the long way back to the parking lot, down the middle downstairs hallway where the English classrooms lined up. He saw a light on at the end of the hallway, a glow coming from the Globe Theatre.

Luke's feet moved a little more quickly when he noticed the light, and he felt the corners of his mouth turn up in a smile.

He remembered last night, the feel of Amanda in his arms, and the taste of the warm coffee on her lips when he finally got up the nerve to kiss her. Luke was one of fewer than two thousand people in the world with a BASE jumping number. He'd taken leaps from buildings, antennae, spans and earth—and had the certificate to prove it.

Some people would regard his stunts as crazy.

But nothing came close to what he felt when he'd held her so close that there was no space between him and Amanda last night. Nothing matched the thrill of closing his eyes and leaning in.

And no jump from a structure, no summit of a peak, and no dive beneath the ocean matched the adrenaline rush he felt not pulling back from the spark they shared in that kiss.

He'd gone crazy alright. Crazy for the Shakespeare-quoting redhead.

Luke kept a steady pace walking down the hall. He was three classrooms away and he realized he couldn't wait to see her.

He opened the door without knocking or hesitating.

"Hey, beautiful." Ok, it wasn't Shakespeare, but it was the honest truth. Amanda Marsh was beautiful, and Luke didn't care if she thought he was crazy for saying so.

"Dr. Baker?" A woman stood up from behind the desk where she'd been picking up the trash can.

"Ivanna?" Luke noticed the large cart on wheels belonging to Port Provident High Schools's beloved custodian, then he saw the small woman standing behind it.

"Are you looking for Miss Marsh? She's been gone a long time."

Luke's heart sank quicker than someone at the end of a bungee cord. "Ok, thanks for letting me know. Have a good night, Ivanna."

She smiled and picked up a new bag to line the trash can with. "You too, Dr. Baker."

Luke headed toward the parking lot, realizing just how much he'd missed not seeing Amanda today. It blew him away how quickly she'd become a fixture in his life.

As he walked toward his car, he noticed an older Toyota executing a shaky three-point turn. As the car pivoted, he caught a glimpse of the driver. When the car came to a stop, he walked up and knocked on the window.

"Violet?"

The teenager rolled down the window, and her ear-to-ear grin shone clearly. "Dr. B. Check it out! This is my Uncle Will. My granny is moving in with him at the end of the month and won't need her car anymore. He was going to sell the car, but when my mom told him about the STEM Academy, he said he'd let me have it if I help out with Granny after school. Isn't that awesome? Now we can send in my application!"

Luke felt a sense of pride. This girl wanted to get to the STEM Academy and her family came together to make it happen. He wished all his students had parents who would move mountains like that.

"Awesome, Violet. Let's get it submitted soon. I know you'll have no problem getting in. This car is going to take you places you've never dreamed."

The man in the passenger seat reached his hand across. Luke stuck his own hand inside the window and shook it.

"Dr. Baker, thank you for believing in Violet. She's always been a smart girl, but no one has pushed her like you have. She'll be the first person in our family to go to college. You don't know what that means to her mother and her granny. And to me. Thank you."

They may have paid out hefty bonuses in Luke's tenure at Global Health and offered matching funds in a 401(k). He knew he'd done quality work there. But nothing compared to this. Nothing compared to changing the entire path of a family, and seeing it face-to-face.

"The pleasure is all mine. Violet's a bright, determined young lady. One of the best students I've taught." He clapped his hand on Violet's shoulder. "Now, go practice that three-point-turn. You've got to be ready to be road-legal."

Violet continued to beam. "Yes sir."

Luke tried to get out of Violet's path before the car started moving again. She needed a little more practice to become a seasoned driver. In spite of checking over his shoulder a few times, he felt good about what this meant for Violet.

But then he started to wonder what this meant for him. And for Amanda. And for The Cupid Caper.

If Violet now had the use of her grandmother's car, then Luke and Amanda no longer needed to pull out all the stops to win the grand prize at the dance.

And if they didn't need to pull out all the stops to win, then he didn't need to put on public displays of Secret Cupid affection.

He didn't need to take Amanda to a high school dance.

And he didn't need to kiss her again.

Except that he did.

And again.

And again.

The fact was, Luke realized as he got in his car and turned the key in the ignition, he'd fallen for Amanda Marsh. And he'd fallen harder for her than he ever thought possible in just a few short days.

He didn't know when his rational, analytical brain had been taken over by poetry and prose and love.

Luke blamed Cupid.

But more than that, he blamed himself for never noticing Amanda's beauty and charm before. He blamed himself for deriding a mock-up of the Globe Theatre when he should have been amazed by the creativity of a teacher who would immerse herself so fully in her work. He blamed himself for writing her off as scurrying from one activity to another instead of seeing someone who cared so deeply for her students and their well-being that she stretched herself far too thin just so she could support them and grow their dreams and knowledge and skills.

And he knew he'd blame himself for the rest of his life if he let Amanda Marsh get away.

But without the cover of The Cupid Caper, how could he tell her that without scaring her off? She'd played along for Violet's sake. Now he needed to convince Amanda that this wasn't a game anymore.

He just didn't quite know how to do that. She'd think he was crazy. Maybe—for the first time in his life—he was. Crazy for the English teacher with a heart of gold.

Luke had been headed to meet some friends for his usual Thursday night pick-up basketball game. But as he drove over to the gym where they played, his mind began to race. Could there be a way to match the orderly scientist who he'd always been with the romantic he knew Amanda needed?

Chapter Six

"WE ARE GOING TO FIND you the perfect dress for Saturday night." Lisa practically squealed out each syllable.

Amanda knew she'd asked Lisa to help her get ready for The Cupid Caper dance...but the minute they got downtown, Amanda regretted that decision. Lisa was taking this far too seriously.

But why? Amanda knew she cared a lot about having one date night out with her co-worker crush. But she couldn't figure out why it meant so much to Lisa.

"Stop." Amanda growled out the word.

Lisa came to a halt in the middle of the sidewalk on Harborview Boulevard and turned her head to the side. "Stop what?"

"This."

"What?"

"You're squealing. You're pirouetting. And you haven't stopped talking long enough to even take a breath. What has gotten into you, Lisa? You know this is all over after the dance anyway. We're just doing this for Violet."

Amanda felt like she'd just heard Poe's raven speak.

Nevermore.

After the weekend, that's all any of this would be—a memory, never to be real feelings and real love.

Except in the one tiny corner of her heart where she'd promised herself she'd hold on to the memories.

"We're doing this for you, Amanda Marsh. Sure, you and Luke are pretending to be all-in on the Cupid Caper for the good of one of your favorite students. But this..." Lisa waved her arm at the shopping district that surrounded them, but kept her gaze fixed steadily on Amanda. "This evening is for you. You deserve your Cinderella moment. Maybe it's a teenage dance in a high school gymnasium instead of a castle with a pumpkin for a carriage and all that. But you're going to look amazing and dance with Luke Baker and have some fun this weekend, simply because you're a wonderful soul who deserves it."

Amanda felt her throat go dry. She wanted to say something back to Lisa but didn't quite know which words to start with. "I didn't know you felt that way, Lisa."

"You're my best friend. I want to see you happy. You give everything to your kids in class and your girls on drill team. I'm the same way with my kids when the curtain goes up. But you know, Amanda...you and I deserve someone cheering in our corners too."

Everything inside melted like a flow of butter over a lobster tail. Amanda pulled Lisa into her arms and hugged her fiercely.

"I don't deserve you," she said.

As Lisa nodded, her chin scooted across the shoulder of Amanda's lightweight sweater. "You are correct. But I don't deserve you, so we're even. Now let's go find your dream dress."

The Purple Pelican, the island's most eclectic boutique, had tied purple balloons to the lampposts in front of the store. Lisa stopped a few steps from the front door.

"I saw a dress in here last week. I really hope it's still on the rack. It's perfect for the Cupid Caper."

Amanda allowed herself to relax into a big smile. Lisa was right. Even if the dream that had been in her head for two years ended at midnight on Saturday, she still deserved to enjoy every moment while it lasted.

She had a good life. She loved her students. She sang in the choir at First Provident Church. She had great friends like Lisa and her other friend Eve, who recently bought an art gallery here on Harborview Boulevard and started a new relationship with Spencer Canley, a connection from her past. She had Mr. Pickles, the world's most ridiculous cat, and was perfectly content when she spent Saturday nights eating ice cream alone while binging romcoms.

Life wasn't flashy, but it was consistent. And she had no complaints.

But maybe she was meant for something just a little bit more.

Even if it would only last until the weekend.

"Show me the dress. I'm totally ready," Amanda said, walking confidently through the door Lisa held open in front of her.

"Hey, Lily!" Lisa waved at her friend Lily Walker as she walked past the counter near the entrance to the boutique. Lily sometimes worked as a substitute in the home economics class at Port Provident High School. "Is that magenta dress from last week still here?"

"The one with the high-low hemline?" Lily stepped down two short stairs and off the elevated platform.

Lisa nodded. "That's the one."

"No, someone bought it on Monday to wear to the Cupid Caper."

"Ugh," Lisa said, ineloquently. "That's what we needed it for."

"I thought you said you weren't going."

"I wasn't planning on it—but then Amanda got nominated. She's got a Cupid crush."

Lily's brow wrinkled a bit. "From a student?"

"No," said Lisa, conspiratorially. "Luke Baker."

"Ooh. He's hot," Lily confirmed as her head nodded in agreement.

"Amanda knows." The timbre of Lisa's voice held more than a hint of teasing.

It was time to diffuse the situation. Quickly. "I thought we were here to see a dress, Lisa Marie."

Lisa held up her hands in surrender. "Fine, fine. We were. But now it's gone. Do you have anything else that's super fun for Amanda?"

"Actually, we do." Lily walked toward a rack at the back of the store. "This."

She plucked at a hanger and held it out in front of Lisa and Amanda. A froth of white lace and enough tulle to make Swan Lake jealous looked crisp and completely over-the-top under the can lights overhead.

"And then it has this hot pink sash." Lily draped an edge of pink that would have made Cupig blush right over the shoulder strap of the dress. "Plus, we have some matching heels that would be perfect."

It was the perfect confection of a dress, but so different than anything Amanda had ever worn in her life. It wasn't

Much Ado About Nothing. Quite the contrary, this dress was definitely something.

"It's so..." Amanda trailed off as she looked at it.

"Capery." Lisa completed Amanda's thought. "You could definitely caper in this. Sold."

Lisa looked at Amanda, eyebrows rising ever higher over wide eyes, imploring her to agree.

She wanted to agree and pull her credit card out of her wallet, but something held her back. "I'm there as a chaperone, Lisa. This dress is about four inches too short for chaperone attire."

A fierce shake of the head came swiftly, cutting off any further thoughts Lisa might have had. "You're a contestant. You've been kissed by Cupid."

"And this might get you kissed by Luke Baker," Lily reasoned.

Amanda took a deep breath and remembered the kiss in the living room. She could feel the pink creeping into her cheeks and hoped she didn't resemble the sash on the dress.

"Looks like that already happened," Lily said, breaking into a smile. "So, this might get you kissed by Luke Baker...again."

There was nothing Amanda hoped for more. She reached in her purse and pulled out a red-and-gold plastic rectangle.

"I'll take it."

LUKE COULD HEAR THE shoes squeaking on the court before he even opened the door to the gym at Provident College. The game had already started.

He was late for a good reason—trying to decide how to make the Cupid Caper last beyond Saturday. Luke had gotten caught up in his thoughts while driving across the island and had wound up taking a very indirect route to the gym.

If only he'd gotten everything sorted out on the drive. Instead, he had more questions than answers.

"Heads up, Baker!" Dane Vasquez, the baseball coach at Provident College, fired a pass straight at Luke's chest.

Luke dropped his bag and instinctively popped his hands up to catch the pass. As he cradled the ball, Luke ran out to the court with his friends.

As the game moved around the court, Luke found himself forcing concentration. Usually, he loved the game. It was a spot in the week to get in some sweat and time with friends. But today, the game was anything but a way to unwind.

"Earth to Baker! You missed another pass, man!" Rigo Vasquez, Dane's cousin and the head of the Port Provident Beach Patrol, laughed as he chided Luke.

Dan Clark, head coach of the Port Provident High School football team, ran past. "Don't worry, boys. He's just been struck by Cupid."

Dane let off a shot and then stopped in the middle of the lane as the orange ball whooshed through the net. "Say what?"

"It's nothing." Luke jogged toward the ball, now bouncing on the sidelines. "Nobody's gonna hustle for the ball?"

"Nope," Dane said. "Not at all, Cupid Boy. Not until you tell us what's going on."

"Guys, it's just a thing for school. Let's get back to the game." Luke stood at the edge of the court, ready to give someone on his team an inbound pass.

Except, judging by the look on every face in front of him, no one was on his team. It was Luke against a group of faces that were not going to move until they heard the details.

All of a sudden, he felt like he'd stepped into some sports-themed retelling of one of Amanda's Shakespearean plays. *Midsummer Night's Rec League? Taming of the Two Point Shot? Two Gentlemen of the Gym?*

"It's just a thing for school. There's a fundraiser that is tied to a dance over the weekend. If you donate, you can do little games and such for your crush—sort of like Secret Santa, but for Valentine's. Someone paired me up with the English teacher and we decided to go along with it because the grand prize is a one-year lease on a car, and we have a student who really needs it so she can get to the STEM Academy next year."

"And that's all there is?" Rigo wiped his brow.

Luke started to nod, then Dan jumped in.

"He bought her a giant Cupid pig doll."

Suddenly, everyone on the court began to laugh.

Luke raised his voice to be heard above the guys. "The grand prize winner is determined by popular vote. We have to convince people."

"With a flying pig?" Rigo said.

"Relax, guys. The day Luke falls for some woman *is* going to be when pigs fly," said Dane.

"I heard she named it Cupig." Dan could barely keep the laughter off his face.

Luke realized his thoughts had finally steered off Amanda—and to how much itching powder he could sneak in the football coach's shoes to enact revenge.

"That's what it said on the tag," Luke said. He could hear a defensive edge creeping into his words.

"*That's what it said on the tag,*" Dan mimicked.

"It doesn't matter anyway, guys. Violet got a car. She just told me. So, Amanda and I don't need to pretend anymore."

Dan got into position, ready to receive the inbound pass and continue the game. He lowered his voice so it didn't carry across the entire court. "But you're not pretending, bro. I can tell. Don't back off. Amanda's special. You should win the Cupid Caper. But not for the car. Do it for you."

Luke punched the ball back across the baseline and into Dan's hands. Dan immediately set into motion, moving toward the basket. Rigo jumped in the lane, trying to block any attempts at a shot.

The similarities became crystal-clear to Luke. He needed to keep driving in the lane. Luke didn't need to let Violet's news block what he knew he had started to feel for Amanda.

Dan did a quick shake and passed the ball back to Luke. Luke moved out of Rigo's reach, then took two steps back and shot a perfect arc toward the goal. The ball touched the edge of the rim then swirled around once, twice, before letting the momentum carry it through the net for a clean score.

The Cupid Caper was his shot.

Luke could only hope Cupid's arrow was as precise as that two-pointer. It had to be. He could stand losing this game—and all the good-natured trash talk from his friends.

But he couldn't lose Amanda.

And he had two days to figure out the right game plan.

STANDING IN THE PARKING lot a block off of Harborview Drive, Amanda stopped next to her car to answer the phone.

"Hello?"

The voice on the other side of the speaker warmed up any lingering chill brought on by the breezy February night.

"Hey, it's Luke. I happened to be up at the school for a second after I got out of my meetings and I noticed a balloon at my desk."

Amanda could feel her face turn red, flushing all the way up to the red roots of her hair.

"Not sure what you're talking about," she teased, trying to play off the giant helium-inflated lips.

"Cupig ratted you out."

Whatever she expected him to say, it wasn't that. "Never trust a pig in a diaper."

"Absolutely not," Luke said with a laugh. "He also told me to see what you were doing tonight. He said you don't need to grade any papers."

"Whew. I'll be sure and let the administration know the pig gave me a pass when my lesson plans aren't turned in for next week."

"They'll understand. That pig has become a bit of a legend at school. So, what *are* you doing tonight?"

Amanda slid her phone between her shoulder and her ear and fumbled to unlock her car without dropping any of the bags from the Purple Pelican. "I'm down on Harborview doing a little shopping, but I was about to head home."

"Isn't there an Italian place right there?"

"Yes, Dal Mare."

"I'm only a few blocks away. Would you like to have dinner?"

She remembered Lisa's words in the boutique earlier. This was for her. The Cupid Caper might come to an end this weekend. But she could keep the memories forever.

All she needed to do was say yes to Luke's question—and not try to overthink it or explain it away.

A smile leapt to her face. There was no sense in even trying to play it cool. "I'd love to. It's also ArtNight down here. How about we meet out front of the gallery on the corner? My friend Eve just bought it, so I think the current owner is having a sale. I'll look around until you get here."

"That'll work. See you in about five minutes or so."

Amanda put the glossy purple bags on the floorboard of her car, then locked the door again. Then she found her steps doing double-time as she practically ran to the gallery, ready to spend an evening with Luke.

"Can't believe they don't have any flying pig art in here."

Amanda turned around with a laugh. Surrounded by original works of art in the gallery, the only thing she had eyes for was Luke.

"Well, I guess we'll just have to take our business elsewhere, Dr. Baker."

His face transformed in an instant. "We will."

"Did I say something wrong?"

Luke shook his head. "No, why?"

"You just look so serious."

Luke slid a hand across the base of her spine, then pivoted Amanda toward the door. "Not serious. Focused."

"Focused?" Amanda still didn't understand. One minute, he was cracking jokes about Cupig, and the next minute, he looked like he was assigning a troublemaker a pass to detention.

"On you." He ushered her across the room. "You're the most beautiful thing in here, you know."

Amanda inhaled deeply, wanting to take in each syllable of Luke's words as fully as she possibly could. "Oh, I don't..."

"I do," he said, cutting off any hint of protest as they left the gallery.

They walked silently for half a block down the sidewalk bordering Port Provident's most historic street, then Luke stopped under an old-fashioned gas lamp that began to flicker with the creeping dusk.

"There's no one else here, Amanda."

He paused before completing his thought, and Amanda blurted out one of twenty thoughts screeching through her mind.

"It's ArtNight. Everyone else is here."

His mouth curled up at one end, and Amanda wanted to slap herself for not controlling her mouth. She just sounded stupid. This man had a Ph.D., for heaven's sake. She knew the Cupid Caper wasn't real. But she didn't want to ruin any minutes she had left in her fairy tale.

"No one we know. This isn't a school function, Amanda. This is you and me. I want to take you to dinner—like a real couple."

Her mouth started running again. "On a date?"

Luke nodded. "I want to take you on a date."

"And?" Amanda couldn't believe that was all. There had to be some kind of clarifying phrase past that. The Cupid Caper was teamwork, a façade they were building in order to help Violet.

Only Amanda's foolish heart was pretending the poems and pigs meant something just a little bit more.

"And I want to kiss you again."

"Here?" Amanda felt the syllable float out breathlessly.

"Anywhere."

Her knees began to soften, but before they had a chance to fully buckle, Luke's arms swept around and pulled her close. As his head lowered to hers, she felt a tingle run down her spine.

Surely it was Cupid's arrow, striking true.

Chapter Seven

FRIDAY STARTED WITH a blur and never slowed down. All day long, the hallways were filled with the smell of roses and a constant buzz of chatter about the weekend's grand finale for The Cupid Caper. Finally, the bell rang and the students all jumped up with more nervous energy than a mug full of coffee topped with a shot of espresso.

"Violet, can you come here for just a second?" Amanda raised her voice to be heard above the din.

Violet slipped against the tide of teenagers and wormed her way to Amanda's desk.

"I've got your essay here. It looks great. Really nice work." Amanda handed a manila filing folder back to Violet, the hard copy of the essay tucked inside. "I made a few minor edits, but overall, there wasn't much I needed to do."

"Thanks again for taking a look at it, Miss Marsh." Violet smiled as she took the folder and slid it into her backpack. "Hey, did Dr. B. tell you about what happened after school yesterday?"

Amanda wrinkled her brow. Luke hadn't been at school yesterday afternoon. She didn't know what Violet was talking about. "No, I don't guess he did."

"I got a car!" A smile leapt onto Violet's normally composed face. "I'm going to get my granny's car once she moves in with my uncle next month. It's older and it's not fancy, but it's going to be mine."

Amanda's jaw dropped slightly and she tried to grind her teeth together to keep Violet from noticing.

"Now I won't have any problems getting to the STEM Academy. Well, that is if I can get in."

"Of course you'll be able to get in. You're exactly the kind of student they're looking for. Congratulations on the car."

She couldn't zone in on the conversation like she wanted to. Amanda felt awful short-changing Violet with a lack of true focus. But a thousand thoughts began to whirr in her mind, like the buzz of a hive of honeybees.

If Violet now had a car, what did that mean for the plan Amanda and Luke had concocted for The Cupid Caper's finale tonight?

And if Luke knew about Violet's new-to-her car, why hadn't he said anything?

The second bell rang. "I've got to run, Miss Marsh. I don't want to miss the bus. Thanks again."

Violet took off out of the classroom at speeds that could best be described as a strong jog. Although plenty of students still conversed in the corridors, Amanda's classroom fell silent.

Except for Amanda's still chaotic thoughts.

She looked at Cupig, sitting in the large chair behind the rectangle table. She remembered how first seeing him perched behind her desk made her smile. She'd loved the fun, romantic gesture, and had even convinced herself that it wasn't just part of some made-up plan.

She'd told herself that if she could only make it through the week, she could find a way to get Luke to see her as more than just the subject of some silly poem.

Against her better judgment, Amanda had allowed herself to begin to think that maybe this was her chance to have one of those moments like in classic literature or fairy tales. She'd thought that it would all be so romantic when it worked out.

Get real, Marsh.

It's not going to work out.

And it never was going to work out.

If she hadn't been sitting in her blue plastic teacher's desk chair, she'd have probably kicked herself—both for her stupidity and for her runaway imagination. Amanda needed Spring Break to hurry up and come. She obviously needed a week off to clear her mind.

Amanda hoped a week would be enough to clear her heart.

Because after Spring Break, Luke Baker wasn't coming back to Port Provident High School. And she was just going to have to be okay with that.

Amanda packed up her bag, then put the fully-loaded canvas tote back in the closet. She wasn't bringing grading home this weekend. She just wanted some downtime.

And maybe a big sampler box of Valentine's Day chocolates.

Hopefully there wouldn't be many caramel ones. She hated the caramel ones. And right now, she just couldn't take sticky disappointment like caramel pretending to be chocolate.

"Amanda?"

Even with her back turned, she knew that voice. She knew it was Luke.

His voice sounded like sticky caramel.

Disappointment.

What happens to a dream deferred, the poet Langston Hughes once asked. She was about to find out. Because her dream of Luke Baker wasn't just deferred. It was done.

Time to face the music.

The stupid, depressing, love song music.

"Oh, hey Luke." She hoped she sounded casual. She certainly felt anything but casual. Her stomach rolled and her head began to throb just above the center of her right eyebrow.

He just stayed at the door—he didn't make a move to come in. Amanda knew what was about to occur next.

"Have you talked to Violet today?"

Amanda tried to steel herself. She visualized her spine turning to shiny metal and she forced her shoulders back out of their slight slouch.

"She was in my last period. I gave her back her essay for the application."

Luke swallowed visibly. "Great. So, did she tell you about the car?"

Amanda's stomach twisted into a tight knot. "She did. How great for her, right?"

She tried to force a cheerful note into her voice, but if it was truly there, she couldn't hear it. She'd gone tone-deaf.

"Absolutely. It's great that her family could arrange that."

"Oh, yeah, great. Absolutely." Amanda had now moved into repetitious blithering.

It wasn't how she wanted to end things with Luke after this wonderful week, but in all honesty, it didn't matter. Things were ending. And there wasn't going to be a good way. It just wasn't possible to break a heart cleanly.

Luke nodded at her stammering statement. "So, I guess this means we're off the hook, right?"

Was he staring at Cupig? She couldn't tell, but she thought so.

Amanda wanted to scream no. She wanted to tell Luke that Violet may have solved her issue, but Amanda hadn't solved her own.

In fact, she'd fallen in deeper than she'd ever thought possible in such a short period of time. When Luke kissed her in her living room, Amanda had seen stars. And then down on Harborview Boulevard, they'd kissed again. She'd felt a breathless rush, like standing on the moon with no air. She'd given in to her fairy tale fantasy because she thought she had a chance to make it come true.

She'd been terribly, terribly wrong. Crazy love, like the fleeting high-octane feelings she made her students read about, were best left in books. It wasn't meant for her.

Amanda choked down the insecurity she feared would pour from her throat and battled her tear ducts to stay shut. "I'll still be there. I'm a chaperone."

Luke nodded, his eyes still on the stuffed pig and not her. It made Amanda feel ridiculous. Here she'd been telling herself she had a shot, but when it all came crumbling down, Luke didn't even want to look at her. He was ignoring her again, just like he had for the last two years.

She should have known better. And she should have never let Lisa convince her that letting down her guard was a good idea.

"I had to work the winter dance, so I'm off the hook for this one." His voice sounded as flat as the commercial-grade of paint on the wall. "I guess if they call our name in the finalists' list, you can tell them we're opting out like Ms. Pantego did."

"Oh, yeah. Sure. I can do that." She'd never felt so small in her life.

Luke straightened and moved a half step from the frame of the door. "Thanks for playing along and being a good sport."

A good sport. Just a game.

A game with her heart.

Of course, he didn't know that. The only person Amanda could blame was herself.

Well, and maybe Lisa and her silly, dramatic bent.

"Violet deserved the best effort. She's a great kid." Amanda needed Luke to leave. Now. Before she did something in front of him that she'd regret even more than giving herself a week of fooling herself that there was something there between her and Luke Baker.

"Absolutely." Luke stuffed one hand into a pocket. "Well, then. I'll see you Monday. Take care of Cupig, ok?"

She could only reply with a feeble gesture; she didn't trust herself to make a sound. Luke took that as his cue to exit the scene.

As she watched him go out of her view, a stage direction from Shakespeare's *A Winter's Tale* came to Amanda's mind.

Exeunt. Pursued by a bear.

Life would not imitate art today.

She wouldn't allow herself to follow, to ask him the questions that were truly on her mind. She wouldn't press to find out if he'd felt the same things in that kiss the other night.

There would be no pursuit of Luke by Amanda. She just needed to accept that Cupid's arrow had missed the mark.

ON SATURDAY, LUKE SAT alone at a candlelit table dinner table set for two.

He had made reservations at Porter's Seafood on his drive home after that first incredible kiss. He'd left Amanda's townhome wondering how he could make something as silly as The Cupid Caper dance into a night she'd never forget. He'd planned to pull out all the stops and then, at the end of the evening, if he saw any flicker of a spark on her part, he'd planned to tell her the truth.

That the Cupid Caper stopped being a joke the minute he really looked at her.

That he'd been caught up in his own world for two years and never really seen her, and he couldn't explain why.

That no reaction he'd ever had a hand in creating within a lab matched the fire he felt when he took her in his arms and kissed her.

But then Cupid got the last laugh and didn't need him anymore. Violet got her car without the need for any silly schemes.

He should have known this would never work. That's why he preferred science. Rules. Order. Even on his pursuits of adventure, he operated with a plan. They weren't folly.

Well, maybe not the BASE jumping.

But he just did those crazy jumps to say that he could, to check a box. He liked checking boxes. Get a result, move on to the next task on the list.

And then Amanda changed that. He realized he wanted to spend a summer night with her—lying on a blanket in the park, listening to her quote sonnets under the stars. He wanted to go to London and see the world through her eyes—not just through a pair of goggles with some attached safety helmet. He wanted to kiss her again, to let time pass without counting anything but the beats of her heart and the staccato of her breathing.

He wanted Amanda.

Luke pushed his glass away with a shove and turned as the waiter walked by.

"Check, please."

THE PULSATING MULTI-colored lights were visible through the narrow windows in the gym door when Luke rounded the corner at the far end of the hallway. He'd heard the thumping of the DJ's music almost as soon as he'd walked in the doors of the school.

Cupid may have badly missed the mark in Luke's own life, but that little diapered cherub sure knew how to throw a party.

"Hey, Dr. B!" Two football players reached up to give Luke a high-five as he walked into the gym. He smiled and played along, but right now, he only had eyes for one person on the Port Provident High campus.

Amanda.

He saw her after only a moment or two of searching. She stood by herself, near the candid photo booth.

She looked like an angel. Cupid would have been proud.

Her red hair had been pulled softly back from her face at the crown and fell across her shoulders in a cascade of curls. The top of her dress appeared to be a fully-lined white lace halter top that tied just at the base of her neck. A sash of hot pink tied around her waist. And the skirt of the dress was made of layer after layer of white tulle and skimmed just above her knees.

Luke drank in the sight of her like bottle after bottle of water at the end of a marathon. Even her hot pink platform heels seemed irresistible to him. He had to remind himself not to charge through the dance floor area and take her into his arms.

Except that he wanted to.

He really, really wanted to.

But now wasn't the right time. She was busy and he didn't want to interrupt. He wanted her focused and all to himself when Luke told her what he needed to say.

He decided to just stay out of the way for a moment, until Amanda had a break in her chaperone duties. He climbed up a set of open bleachers and found himself a seat about two-thirds of the way up and settled in to watch the scene below.

Liz Langton stepped in front of the DJ's set up and grabbed a microphone.

"Port Provident High, are you ready to cast your vote for the winners of the Cupid Caper?"

A cheer erupted from the assembled students. They'd been waiting for this.

"I'm going to call out the names of the finalists," the assistant principal continued. "If I call your name, make your way to the front. Then we'll have the vote for the best couple."

Even without the blaring music from the DJ, the sound levels in the room remained high on the decibel chart.

"Mike O'Connell, Laura Blake, Cara Percy, Peter Stephenson. You are all finalists in The Cupid Caper." Applause and whistles and cheers broke out. The students parted, clearing little stream-like paths for their friends to make it to the front. "Congratulations. You've completed all the challenges of The Cupid Caper and were selected by the Student Council committee to compete for a chance to win that one-year lease on a new car that was so graciously donated to the school. And we have one more pair to come up front. Their inclusion this year was a little unorthodox, but Student Council voted to name them finalists as well."

A tingling sensation kicked Luke in the gut. He knew this feeling. He got it every time he was about to make a jump or take on a new adventure.

He knew what Liz Langton was about to say before she even finished her explanation.

"Welcome to the stage our last couple, Luke Baker and Amanda Marsh!"

Luke saw Lisa Fleming poke at Amanda, who just waved her hands. He could see Amanda's lips moving, but the noise in the room drowned out what she was saying.

Except he knew what she was doing. He needed to do something before she was heard.

They might not be trying to win that car anymore, but Luke wanted to win a prize much more valuable. He remembered Lisa's words about Amanda's high expectations and her being in love with love.

If Amanda wanted the fairy tale, he would give it to her.

He stood up and cupped his hands around his mouth.

"But soft! What light through yonder gymnasium breaks? It is The Cupid Caper, but Amanda is the sun!"

Several hundred heads turned at once to look at the corner of the bleachers. Luke only cared about the reaction of one.

His heart raced, partly from the stunt he'd just pulled. But partly because he didn't know how Amanda would react.

She stood in front of the bleachers, drop jawed.

It still wasn't clear what was running through Amanda's mind. But Luke figured the adage of "in for a penny, in for a pound" rang true in this instance. At least if he lost Amanda, he'd know he'd pulled out all the stops he could.

He could see a few drops of wetness collecting in the corners of her eyes as he stair-stepped down the rows of bleachers.

Oh no. He'd embarrassed her in front of her students.

"Luke? What are you doing?" Even though the gym full of students had fallen largely quiet in order to follow the unfolding drama, he could barely hear Amanda's words.

"The fairy tale, Amanda. I know you want the fairy tale." Luke reached his hand out to Amanda and hoped against hope that she'd take the offering.

She delicately placed her palm in his and a flood of memories from the other night came crashing back as he touched her soft skin again. He tried to focus and not trip over the last bleacher.

"Shall we?"

She nodded, but the glisten of tears was still there and he didn't know what to do about it. He wanted to kiss them away.

But not in front of all the kids. He wouldn't do that to her.

Luke guided Amanda through the crowd and he could hear the tapping of Lisa's heels following closely behind. As they neared the front of the expansive room, the students started to cheer and whistle again.

Even if Amanda appeared completely unsure of the idea, it seemed the students liked what they were seeing.

"Dr. Baker. Miss Marsh." The assistant principal couldn't contain her grin. "As I said, you were both a very unorthodox addition to The Cupid Caper. But thanks to a very generous donation from the Port Provident Baccheus Society that completely funded several scholarships for our Student Council leadership to attend the annual Student Government Congress held this summer at the University of Texas, we didn't feel that we could turn your entry form away. Four students will be attending the program because of four entries funded in The Cupid Caper. Unfortunately, the other two teachers were not able to participate. But I was glad to see the two of you having some fun with it. Nice work on the giant pig, Dr. Baker."

"His name is Cupig, Ms. Langton. But what is the Port Provident Baccheus Society? It seems a little strange to have a high school club named for the Roman god of wine."

A throat cleared behind them. "Baccheus is also the Roman god of the theatre."

Amanda's head snapped around. She flinched and gripped Luke's hand tightly "Lisa? You actually did this? After I told you not to?"

"I love a good love story," she said simply, without remorse or apology. "And luckily, so does Ms. Langton."

The assistant principal spoke up before Amanda could get her next words out. "Well, well. Let's just vote, shall we? Mike O'Connell, you're first. Tell our voters why you should win The Cupid Caper. As you know, the winner will be voted on by the crowd's applause."

Lisa walked in a wide circle behind Amanda and picked up a giant thermometer-looking prop.

"Thank you, Ms. Fleming. You can work the applause meter."

Lisa just grinned like a child at a birthday party.

"So, Mike? Tell us why you picked Laura to be your secret Cupid."

The basketball forward towered over the petite cheerleader. "Well, Ms. Langton, she's come to all our games this year and cheered for us, and I don't think we'd be going to the district playoffs without her support. She makes me want to play better."

Mike leaned way down and gave Laura a peck on the cheek as the other basketball players and cheerleaders led the rest of the students in celebration for the first couple.

Luke couldn't even focus on what was going on as the next couple had their turn. This time, it was the girl who had picked the guy. She told a little story about sitting behind him in math class, but as she spoke, Luke zoned out.

His fingers still wrapped around Amanda's hand. She stood still and quiet. Luke wished he could read her mind. He'd seen the tears earlier and couldn't help but think the worst. But he knew he needed to follow through.

Luke knew no experiment was complete until you'd worked through the steps and drawn the conclusions. No scientist just acted on hypothesis alone.

So, he would take the microphone and say what he needed to say.

If it backfired on him, well, he'd just stay hidden in his lab for the next two weeks until Spring Break and his transition to his new role.

"And finally, our third couple. Dr. Baker, should we have Ms. Fleming do the honors, since she's the one who filled out your entry cards and wrote your initial poems?" The carefully-coiffed blonde held out the microphone in Lisa's direction.

"No, that's ok. I'll do it." Luke braced himself for the leap. He reached for the microphone with one hand and gave Amanda's palm a slight squeeze with the other.

She squeezed back.

"Amanda, I know I tried to toss that poem in the trash. Thank you for saving it. Neither of us knew it at the time, but that one simple act saved me. My whole life, I've analyzed things to death. Even love. I thought this would just be a role to play for a week—like an actor in one of those Shakespeare plays you love to quote. But it's made me realize there's a role I want to play for the rest of my life. It's the role that's by your side."

He reached the hand with the microphone out, but kept his eyes focused on hers. The gray in her irises retreated as the deep emerald green spread from pupil to the edge of the center boundary.

Amanda gave a shy smile. "'My bounty is as boundless as the sea, My love as deep; the more I give to thee, The more I have, for both are infinite.'"

"More Shakespeare? *Romeo and Juliet*?"

She nodded. "Of course."

"Does your friend Shakespeare say anything about Cupid?"

"As a matter of fact he does. 'Love goes by haps; Some Cupid kills with arrows, some with traps.' That's actually from *Much Ado About Nothing*, though."

"I think Lisa intended this to be a trap." Luke flicked his eyes up at the drama teacher hovering behind her best friend's shoulder. "But it seems Cupid's arrow flew true. I've definitely fallen in love with you, Amanda Marsh. And no matter who gets the most applause here at The Cupid Caper, as long as you walk out of here with me, I know I'm the real winner."

The tears sprang up in Amanda's eyes again, but they didn't fall. He could feel a slight tremble in her arm as he continued to hold her hand.

"I'd decided that the stories, as pretty as they sounded, were all nonsense. Nothing like that truly happened in real life. But this, this seems more like a dream, Luke."

"It's your fairy tale, Amanda. You believed in love long before I did and you taught me what it meant. You deserve this." He gestured at the crowd with his free hand. "And this."

Luke leaned over and threaded his free hand in the waves of red hair at the top of Amanda's neck. Then slowly, he lowered his head and touched his lips to Amanda's.

A roar went up from the crowd. Hoots and screams rang off the rafters high in the ceiling. And the combustion that ignited between him and Amanda erupted into a flame.

They'd never hear the end of it from the students, but Luke didn't care. When Amanda wrapped her arm around Luke's shoulders and pulled herself closer, he knew she felt the same way.

"Look at that applause meter, Port Provident!" Ms. Langton had to shout into the microphone to be heard. "It's off the charts! I think we have a winner."

Luke pulled himself away from Amanda for just a moment. "I don't think we'll be needing the car, Ms. Langton, so you can choose another winner. But if you don't mind, I'd like to see if you can get a replacement chaperone. I missed getting to take this lovely lady out to dinner tonight, and I'd like to make up for that."

"Of course, Dr. Baker."

With permission granted, Luke smiled down at Amanda. "What do you say, Miss Marsh?"

"You can just call me Juliet."

Luke looked down at their hands, still locked together. He never wanted to let go. "Well, then, Juliet. Let's see where Cupid's wings fly us to next."

You Don't Have to Leave Port Provident!

Start Lucky in Love Now!

All Lisa Fleming, Port Provident High School's theatre teacher, wants for Spring Break is peace and quiet. But her Nana has other plans—and they include a white chapel in Las Vegas. Lisa must form an unlikely alliance with disillusioned Vegas legend Ryan "Lucky Charm" McBride if she's going to have any chance of stopping this far-fetched wedding and getting Nana on a plane back to Port Provident. But is Ryan the lucky charm she needs to find true love of her own? Continue the Holiday Hearts series and find out if what happens in Vegas can make it all the way back to everyone's favorite Texas beachside town.

Start reading Lucky in Love today!
www.books2read.com/LuckyInLoveBook

COULD A LUCKY CHARM SHE NEVER KNEW SHE NEEDED BE THE KEY TO TRUE LOVE?

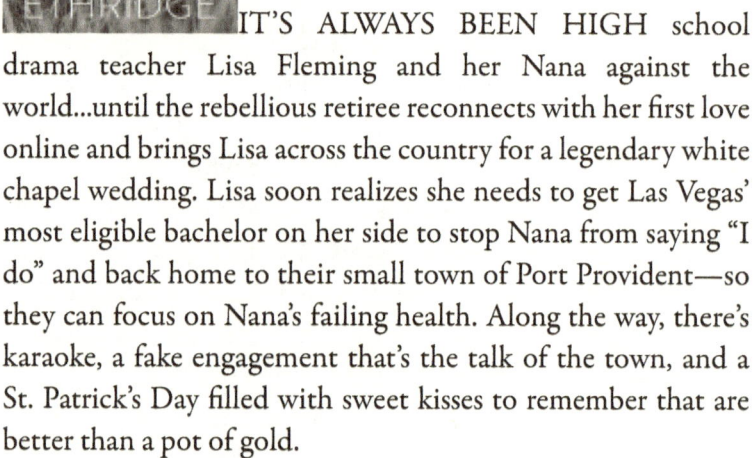

IT'S ALWAYS BEEN HIGH school drama teacher Lisa Fleming and her Nana against the world...until the rebellious retiree reconnects with her first love online and brings Lisa across the country for a legendary white chapel wedding. Lisa soon realizes she needs to get Las Vegas' most eligible bachelor on her side to stop Nana from saying "I do" and back home to their small town of Port Provident—so they can focus on Nana's failing health. Along the way, there's karaoke, a fake engagement that's the talk of the town, and a St. Patrick's Day filled with sweet kisses to remember that are better than a pot of gold.

If you love quick, sweet escape romance stories filled with hope, heart, and happily-ever-after that will make you swoon and leave you with a smile, you will want to celebrate the holidays with the residents of the beachside small town of Port Provident.

__www.books2read.com/LuckyInLoveBook__

Join Kristen's Reader Community Today and Receive a Free Port Provident Story

Join Kristen's reader community today for the latest and get A Place to Find Love, *a sweet escape romance that introduces you to Port Provident, Texas and the residents who find love on the island, for free!*
www.kristenethridge.com/newsletter[1]

Sneak Peek: Lucky in Love—Chapter One

"POPS, THERE'S NO WAY you're convincing me you brought those for the USO lounge."

Ryan McBride nodded his head in the direction of the two dozen roses, wrapped in cellophane and tissue and tied with an oversized crimson-red bow.

Ryan caught a glance at Pops, who looked like he won the Miss America pageant. That explanation seemed just as ridiculous as this last-minute trip to the florist and then the airport—since Ryan knew neither had anything to do with America's heroes. That much was as clear as the plastic sheet surrounding the bouquet.

Bill McBride climbed in the car and sat down, careful not to crush the flowers as he buckled his seatbelt. "I support our troops, Ryan."

"I didn't say you didn't, Pops. I know you do. You've been one of them and had their back ever since." Ryan let his eyes leave the road long enough to give his grandfather a stern stare. "But usually when I bring you to the airport to welcome home our troops, you let a 'thank you' and a handshake suffice. And you usually wear your American Legion cap. Not a tie. Pops, don't lie to me. What's going on here?"

Bill stared ahead stoically, seemingly considering his words before he spoke as they made their way down Interstate 15 to McCarron International Airport.

Ryan decided he would just let Pops have the next word. Ryan read the bluffs of others for a living, a very lucrative living.

And he'd just called Pops's bluff. He had Pops, and the old man knew it.

"Well," Pops dragged out the syllable, still unwilling to commit to revealing whatever he had up his starched long sleeve.

"*Mmm-hmm?*"

"You see, I'm meeting someone there." Then he added hastily, "Not a service member, though."

"I figured that one out already, Pops. Keep going." Ryan turned into the main entrance to the airport. "What airline, Pops?"

"American. She's coming from Texas." Pops pointed at the sign just ahead, which directed them to the terminal where American Airlines landed. "Ok, so, keep going. What's her name?"

Pops bent his head low, smelling the flowers, almost as though he was enjoying the perfume worn by his mystery woman.

Ryan snuck another glance at Pops. When had he had time to meet a woman? And especially one from Texas? When Bill had moved to the retirement community a year ago, Ryan half expected him to find companionship over the Friday night bingo cards.

But Texas?

Something wasn't adding up.

Was it possible that Pops wasn't playing with a full deck anymore?

And while Ryan didn't understand the whole situation right now, he did understand odds. And the odds of his ninety-two-year-old grandfather meeting a woman from halfway across the country were virtually non-existent.

"Gina Mae," Pops lowered his voice and ran the syllables together into a mumble. "Her name is Gina Mae Lee. Well, Gina Fleming now. But back when I knew her, she was Gina Mae Lee. And she was something."

A career as a card shark had made Ryan mostly immune to displays of emotion. Emotion got you burned. Emotion opened the door to letting someone take advantage of you.

Emotion was for losers.

"Ok, Pops. Gina Mae Something from Texas is coming to visit. And you got her flowers." Ryan swung into a parking space and put his sports car in park. "Why?"

Pops turned his head toward the window, and stared as though he was seeing another time and another place.

"Because she's getting ready to become Mrs. Bill McBride, and every gal deserves something special on her wedding day. Especially my gal."

"Your gal, Pops?" Ryan finally let emotion sneak out in his words. "This is a little ridiculous, don't you think? First you tell me we're going to greet the troops. Then you come out carrying an entire florist's shop, and now you're marrying some girl with a bunch of names at the airport?"

Ryan couldn't figure out why Pops was trying to deceive him. Their relationship had been built on trust and honesty, for as long as Ryan could remember.

Bill cut off Ryan's questions. "She's not some girl with a bunch of names. She was my first love. And she'll be my last. You've got a cynic's heart. You'll never understand."

Bill placed a defiant hand on the door latch and gave it a strong pull that was more Chuck Norris than Chuck E. Cheese.

"Won't understand? First love, last love, huh? Where does Memaw fit in? Did you forget about the woman you were married to?"

Pops stopped his exit from the car and turned to look right at Ryan. His fluffy white eyebrows lowered like fanciful caterpillars over his ice-blue eyes. "She's been gone since you were four, Ryan. And that's a long time to live with nothing but memories, when all you want is a hand to hold. I doubt I have five more years on this earth, youngster. I'm going to make my time count. And that's exactly what she told me to do, for your information."

He put one leg deliberately out of the car, then stood carefully, cradling the riot of red blooms like a newborn baby. "And whether you stay or leave me to call a taxi to take me and my bride back to town, you'll never speak so disrespectfully to me again, young man. Do you hear?"

Ryan took in a slow breath. If he didn't back off, Pops was going to take a cab to a little white chapel.

"I hear, Pops. I don't get any of this. But I hear you."

"Good. Then let's get going. Gina Mae's never been to Las Vegas. I don't want to make her wait in a crowded airport by herself."

Ryan watched Pops stand a little taller as he walked to the door. He had moved Pops out here to the desert southwest to try and improve his health and quality of life. Sadly, it seemed like nothing had made much of a difference...until this moment.

Ryan followed his grandfather's eager steps through the airport. He scooted around women toting pink rhinestone doggy carriers. He slid past groups of men slapping each other on the back and gearing up for a bachelor party. He ducked out of the way of tall blondes with fake tans and faker female features, the Playboy-cloned girls looking to make it big at some club, some hotel, some limelight.

Everything Ryan saw as they walked made sense to him. They were all part of the biggest stereotypes about Vegas.

The only thing head scratcher was everything Pops had just told Ryan. He couldn't make sense of how this all happened and Ryan never suspected a thing. Wasn't he supposed to watch for "tells"—those little behaviors that signaled something to come?

Maybe he was losing his touch.

But he would make damn sure he wasn't going to lose Pops.

Ryan McBride didn't know a thing about Gina Mae What's-Her-Name. But he knew he'd protect his grandfather from lions, tigers, bears...and gold diggers.

Which was about the only explanation Ryan could come up with for flying halfway across the country and marrying someone you hadn't seen in decades. Every other explanation defied logic. And logic and odds ruled Ryan's life. He always went where the logic led. Let others be led by gut feelings. Ryan McBride hadn't gotten to the top of one of the highest-stakes games in the world by trusting his feelings.

Right now, he didn't trust Pops' feelings, either.

"There she is, son!" Pops raised his arms and waved the flowers furiously over his head. "Gina Mae!"

Ryan saw a diminutive tuft of white hair coming their way. The little walking cotton ball didn't look like much of a threat. But Ryan had seen enough bluffs at the tables to know things weren't always what they seemed.

IF WHAT HAPPENED IN Vegas was supposed to stay in Vegas, then Lisa Fleming wasn't happening.

Because she sure as Cirque du Soleil wasn't staying here.

And neither was Nana. Nana just didn't know it yet.

But since the moment Lisa had come home from her last day of teaching high school before Spring Break and Nana had handed her a plane ticket to Las Vegas, then blurted out a hare-brained scheme that she'd re-connected with her first childhood love on social media, Lisa had felt like she had joined a movie with the National Lampoon's squad about the worst vacation ever.

But, no. That wasn't enough. As soon as the flight attendant served Nana a tiny glass of overpriced wine, Nana had to go and drop the Nana bomb.

She wasn't just going on vacation to see the fountains at the Bellagio or to waste Lisa's inheritance one shiny coin at a time in a nickel slot machine.

Nope, Nana announced she was getting married in a Vegas chapel to her early-days-of-World-War-II sweetheart.

In that moment, Lisa had flagged down the flight attendant and ordered a tiny bottle of whatever the airline was serving. And now, with every step she took through the airport, she wished she'd ordered one for the road. Or the terminal. Or the baggage claim. Or whatever.

Nana was over ninety years old. Lisa couldn't keep her from going on a trip. But somewhere over New Mexico, empowered by that teeny-tiny adult beverage, Lisa decided she *could* keep Nana from making the biggest mistake of her life.

It was completely possible for Nana to go to Vegas and catch up with an old friend.

She just didn't have to marry him, for Pete's sake.

And if that meant giving up a nice, relaxing Spring Break to ensure that Nana, the woman who protected Lisa her whole life, stayed away from little white Vegas wedding chapels—then so be it.

Once safely past small airport lounges filled with cigarette smoke and dreams of jackpots, Nana gained speed. Lisa found herself trying to keep up with Nana's imitation of the Senior Olympics track squad. Then, once she'd cleared baggage claim, Nana sprinted toward a gentleman in a perfectly starched dress shirt and fell straight into his arms as though she had tripped and landed there.

As they stayed locked in a warm embrace, Lisa began to feel as though she were intruding. They were surrounded by strangers and serenaded by the sounds of luggage carousels, but still Lisa like an outsider at this moment that had been more than six decades in the making.

She'd never had a relationship that had been more than six months in the making.

Lisa looked over Nana's shoulder and above the white-haired man's softly bent head.

She couldn't miss the sight of midnight blue eyes, black hair, and a chiseled chin locked in a light dusting of yesterday's beard. Of all the people in this busy airport, the man behind the couple-of-the-moment had caught her attention.

The way he was staring at Nana and her friend made Lisa uncomfortable, like when she watched scary movies and knew something was about to happen just by the music.

"Are you waiting on something?" Lisa could hear the shortness in her own voice come out like the lead housewife on a catty reality show. "You can just get your suitcase and move on, you know."

He narrowed his eyes. "Can't."

"Didn't your mother teach you staring was rude?"

"Nope."

Ugh. Did the man know how to put two syllables together? Lisa's inner diva had reached a fast, bubbly boil. There was nothing she could do to prevent what was about to happen.

"Well, she should have. I can correct that right now, if you'd like."

That was her Grade-A teacher voice. The beast had been unleashed. No going back now. Mr. Annoying needed to get his suitcase and head for the exit.

"Not really."

Well, at least he used more than one syllable. The Grade-A teacher in her appreciated that.

Her eyes unlocked from his and swept downward.

Whoa, diva... Now Lisa's inner teacher was speaking directly to her, reminding her that this was no time to appreciate any of his finer qualities. Not his syllables...or anything else.

He might have been nice to look at, but his manners didn't match his looks. "There are plenty of taxis outside just waiting to take you wherever you need to go. This is a private moment."

Before Mr. Midnight Eyes could reply, the older gentleman pulled two steps back out of the embrace with Nana.

"He can't go get a taxi. He *is* the taxi," Bill said. "Gina Mae, this is my grandson, Ryan McBride."

Ryan tilted his head toward the reunited couple, in a wordless form of greeting.

Cocky jerk. He could have just answered her original question. She'd just used her teacher voice for nothing.

"Well, isn't that fun?" A smile came over Nana's face and she gestured back at Lisa. "Bill, this is my great-granddaughter, Lisa Marie."

Ugh. Every time Nana said that, Lisa felt like she was about to be painted on velvet and hung up at Graceland.

Lisa held her palm up and tried to deflect. "Lisa. Lisa will do."

The world was only big enough for one Lisa Marie in a town with an Elvis impersonator in every white chapel on every corner.

Bill McBride walked over to Lisa and picked up her hand. He lifted it and gave a short peck just over the crest of the knuckles. "Pleased to meet you, my dear. Thank you for bringing my Gina Mae safely to me."

The sincerity with which Bill spoke touched Lisa's heart and made her feel a little guilty for having zero intention of abandoning her plan to circumvent this wedding somehow and get back to this airport as quickly as possible in order to go home.

But since her Nana had always been a big believer in the adage that said you get more flies with honey than vinegar, she was willing to be sweet for now. Goodness knows Nana had drilled the concept into Lisa's head over the years.

She packed up the teacher voice.

"If I'd known we were meeting a true gentleman like you, we'd have been here sooner," Lisa said with a smile. Honestly, the groom-to-be held an irresistible charm, like a chivalrous teddy bear.

Nice to know there were men like that in the world. Too bad they were all ninety years old.

Lisa could feel the stare of Bill's grandson from his staked-out spot just a few feet away. *Sooo.* The apple fell pretty far from Bill McBride's gallant tree.

Too bad. Those eyes would have been a perfect complement for chivalry. Wasn't blue the color of something knightly? Lisa couldn't remember the old stories. She left those things to her friends in the English department.

But hey, it wasn't like Lisa had time to flirt anyway.

She needed to save Nana from herself, her crazy plans, her long-suspected memory issues, and one well-mannered teddy bear who was probably in the same synapse-induced twilight that Nana was.

"Shall we go? Ryan, can you grab my sweetheart's bags? Her hands are full." Bill smiled first at Gina Mae and then at the oversized puff of flowers she could barely fully grasp with her arthritic fingers.

"Sure, Pops." Ryan reached behind his grandfather and plucked the handle of Nana's rolling suitcase. "Got it."

Mr. Blue Eyes was a man of few words. Hopefully, his apparent lack of interest meant he wouldn't be in her way the next few days as she brought some balance back to Nana's life.

"You need any help?" Ryan McBride's voice reminded her of caramel. Low, slow, and with just a hint of burnished sweetness. Now that he'd uttered several syllables together, his voice surprised Lisa. After years in the world of the theater, listening for tone and inflection in the spoken word came as second nature. It was just an analysis she made without even really thinking about it.

His candied voice made Lisa's stomach growl a little as it made her blood pressure rise a few notches with the awareness of it.

Lisa shook her head. "I've got it." At least she could confidently say she had one thing under control here.

Nana and Bill took the lead, walking toward the doors that led to the parking lot with the lightness of step most commonly seen in teenagers. Lisa couldn't believe it. Nana had moved in with her two years ago when it became clear that the day-to-day tasks of keeping a house cleaned and maintained, and dinner cooked, and laundry washed were just taking a physical toll on her. But now, here in the middle of Las Vegas, holding hands with her long-lost first love, it seemed like the years had just disappeared—from both the calendar and her arthritic knees.

The transformation amazed Lisa, and she tried to keep herself from looking obviously drop-jawed as she followed the newly reunited couple.

Standing directly behind Ryan McBride forced Lisa to keep her potentially drop-jawed state in check, too.

He wore a plain black T-shirt and a pair of jeans that seemed dyed to match the black-blue of his eyes. The shirt and the jeans both seemed to fit him like a casual second skin, careless yet confident at the same time.

Snap out of it, Lisa Marie. The only thing she needed to be confident of right now was making sure that her Nana escaped Vegas without making decisions she clearly didn't think all the way through. Nana needed help, and Lisa couldn't risk a wrong move by being distracted.

Her toe collided with six inches of brightly painted concrete that divided two handicapped parking spots. Lisa flailed her left arm a bit, trying to regain balance. Her suitcase landed with a thud as she jerked it over the offending curb.

Quickly, she lifted her chin up to see if anyone noticed.

Ryan raised an eyebrow.

Lisa took a deep breath in through her nose, resisting the challenge. Yep, she had everything under control.

Or not.

But she was darned sure gonna fake it 'til she made it. No one in Las Vegas would notice a little more fake, would they?

WHEN THEY ALL GOT TO the car, Ryan realized immediately he had a big problem on his hands. His fancy European sports car really wasn't made to chauffeur four grown adults, two suitcases, two carry-on bags, two purses, and one oversized bouquet of roses.

He ran a hand through his hair in a swipe of frustration. He loved Pops, but everything about today had been crazy. If Pops had just been honest with him, maybe they could have made plans for transportation with an adequate number of seats and square feet of trunk space. If Pops had come clean from the start, maybe they wouldn't have been in this predicament at all. Because Ryan would have tried every negotiation skill at his disposable to talk Pops out of this craziness.

Which Pops obviously knew, the crafty old man.

And so, that brought Ryan to standing outside a black convertible sports car in a parking garage, wondering how everything—including the accompanying cast of characters—was going to wedge in there.

"Pops? Where are we going? I'm not taking these ladies back to your retirement home, am I?"

"Well, of course not, Ryan. It's not a hotel. I made Gina Mae a reservation at your place. In the honeymoon suite." Pops' eyes lit up with an arctic twinkle.

"At my place? You mean the Renaissance Grand?" The honeymoon suite at the newest and most talked about hotel on the Vegas strip did not come cheap.

Pops nodded as he opened the door. "Yes, sir. I put my girl there because I thought you'd be able to help her if she needed anything. She wasn't sure her great-granddaughter would come, but since she's here now, maybe you can help me with getting her a room too."

"Wait. Don't get in the car yet. I'm not sure how everything's going to fit, Pops." He popped open the trunk and picked up the first suitcase, trying a few different angles to get them to both fit. His game of suitcase Tetris worked, but barely.

With that task completed, Ryan turned his attention back to Pops and the limited space inside the car.

"So, can you help me get another room at your place, Ryan?" Pops leaned over and slid the seat forward, then started to help Gina Mae into the half-sized back seat.

Out of the corner of his eye, Ryan noticed Gina Mae's great-granddaughter standing cautiously to the side. Clearly, she didn't want to get in Pops' way, but she wasn't convinced her assistance was not going to be needed. Ryan recognized the skeptical half-scowl on her face because it was written across his own. He could feel his eyebrows knitted into a quirky furrow.

"Your place?" The skepticism wasn't just pasted on her face. It was woven through her voice too. "Do you own the hotel or something?"

Ryan had lived out under the glittering lights of Vegas long enough to automatically read into that statement. In this world, things were so often not what they seemed. And that included a long-lost girlfriend and her tag-along great-granddaughter.

Ryan hated that "gold digger" popped into his mind immediately. But he'd been trained a long time ago to look for signs and to anticipate the next move and then the next, and the next, so on until he reached the end game.

Why would some Social Security recipient find his grandfather online and drag along her great-granddaughter on this trip? Gina Mae seemed sincere and her great-granddaughter looked a little overwhelmed. But in this stop in the Nevada desert, things just were rarely what they seemed.

Everyone had a story.

And everyone knew that what happened in Vegas stayed in Vegas.

Except this time. Ryan knew something didn't add up. He knew these two would not be staying in Vegas. They were on the next plane back to Texas, even if he had to charter a flight himself.

"Ryan?" Pops's voice had the bark of a drill sergeant.

"Yeah?" Ryan answered without thought, still trying to make sense of what was going on.

"The young lady asked you a question. Are you going to reply?"

Pops's tone and words made Ryan feel very small. He hadn't been taken down a notch in a long time. As the winner of the last four consecutive Global Poker Challenge rings, most people in this town knew who Ryan McBride was. And they all treated him with a champion's deference.

"No, it's not my hotel. I just live there." Ryan looked over the convertible top of the car at the woman with the honey blond curls that fell over her shoulders and trailed down her back. "Pops? What are you doing?"

Bill ducked his head low and squished like a crab into the narrow back seat of the car.

"Sitting with my sweetheart. Is that okay?"

Ryan pushed his hand through his hair again. He usually carefully controlled all physical signs of emotion, reluctant to ever tip off an opponent. It was a key to playing good poker.

Good thing he was not at a table this afternoon. There was no way he could ever have concealed everything he thought about this whole crazy trip.

"Sure, Pops. I just didn't think you two would fit comfortably back there. I'm not even sure that seat is made to hold preschoolers."

"Well, I wouldn't say it's comfortable, but we'll do." Bill squeezed the hand of the woman next to him and looked in her eyes with a relaxed smile. "Right, Gina Mae?"

Her smile bookended his. "Right as rain, Bill. My flowers are a bit squashed, though. Lisa Marie, get in the car and hold these, will you?"

Ryan saw Lisa exhale sharply. "Sure, Nana. Pass them up."

Lisa ducked and slid into the front seat, then moved it up to give some more room to the cramped passengers in the back seat. She laid the proffered bouquet in her lap. Ryan caught a glimpse of her as he started the car and adjusted the volume on the radio. Between the curly hair, pinned up in a clip at the crown of her head, and the oversized riot of flowers, Lisa looked like an exasperated beauty queen.

In a town where most of the beauty was exactly as the adage said—skin deep—something about Lisa's soft features made Ryan do a brief double-take. He wasn't used to seeing a woman with no makeup and her hair carelessly secured with a plastic clip. For all that he didn't understand why she was here or what her endgame would wind up proving to be, something about her was refreshing.

Ryan mentally slapped himself as he backed out of the parking space. It was never just about the chips your opponent put on the table or the cards they showed.

It was always about the endgame.

And until Ryan McBride knew what Lisa Marie Fleming and her little great-grandmother were up to, then he needed to stay on top of his own game so he and Pops didn't come up with the losing hand.

No mental lapses. No loss of concentration. No signs that gave away his thoughts.

And no second glances at a clean, fresh face framed by some spiral waves of honey and brown sugar.

"MR. MCBRIDE. IT'S GOOD to see you." A uniformed man opened the door as they pulled under the valet porte-cochere at the Renaissance Grand. Another uniformed man materialized at Lisa's door and swung it open, then helped her get out.

What in the name of Velvet Elvis were they wearing? Were those pantaloons?

Lisa narrowed her gaze, studying the strips of red and black and gold fabric fashioned into some kind of bubble shorts.

There were tights.

And feathers in floppy velvet berets.

She was looking at both of the freaking gentlemen of Verona. Good grief. Wait until she told her best friend Amanda—the English teacher back at Port Provident High School who loved all things Shakespeare.

Lisa stood back and looked at everything else surrounding her. Shades of red and gold and black set the tone for the entire entrance. The floor into the main lobby was black marble, polished to a high shine. A red carpet rolled out to the edge of the sidewalk. Lisa walked over to it to wait out of the way of the hustle and bustle. She remembered attending the Tony Awards years ago, stunned by all the glitter, spotlights, and theater royalty.

That night felt special, otherworldly. She had to admit that the Renaissance Grand felt much the same right now.

This was definitely like no other world she'd ever seen.

She'd been sucked into some parallel-universe-other-dimension-time-warp thing.

But she couldn't lose her focus on the one thing that did make sense: getting Nana on the next possible plane back to Texas.

And while she was at it, Lisa silently thanked the little twinkling stars on the fake Da Vinci-styled ceiling above her that there were no men in velvet berets in Texas.

"Nana? Are you okay?" Lisa called to her great-grandmother, being gently escorted to the red carpet by one of the Veronian-style doormen on one side, and Bill on the other. The uniformed man who'd opened Ryan's door grabbed both of the suitcases effortlessly, and as they neared the valet station, Lisa saw Ryan hold out a small roll of green-and-cream bills as a note of thanks.

"Should we take your car over to the residences garage, Mr. McBride, or will you be coming back for it soon?" The man with the suitcases reached out, took the tip, and discreetly tucked them in his pocket.

"Go ahead and take her back to my space, Kip. I'm playing in the celebrity lead up to the charity tournament tonight. It'll be a short walk home."

"Charity tournament?" Ryan's grandfather turned with an emotional reaction. "Ryan, our rehearsal dinner is tonight. You've got to come with us."

Ryan came up alongside his grandfather as Gina Mae hesitated behind them slightly. "Pops, I've been booked to play tonight for months. You've kind of sprung this whole wedding bells scenario on me in just the last hour or so, and I still don't quite understand why you kept this all a secret. Where are you having dinner? What time?"

The gentleman stopped and leaned up against the first black marble pillar just inside the door. "Well, I don't have a place yet. I was hoping you could recommend something. You know all the best places here."

"Pops, I know a lot of great places. And the best are booked well in advance." Ryan looked toward the corner of the room, then continued to follow the man with the suitcases to the reception desk. "Which I might could have helped you with if you'd given me a heads up about your plans."

Bill looked at Ryan and gave him a shrug, then looked down at the floor. "You'd have talked me out of it, Son. I didn't want you calculating the odds," he said, the words almost falling under his breath. Bill waited for Gina Mae to catch up. Once her hand was firmly in his again, they both followed in Ryan's wake.

Lisa trailed behind, feeling no hurry to get checked in. Despite the anachronistic Veronians, the hotel was beautiful. Shiny, bold colors were everywhere. The decoration was impeccable and modern yet with a strong Italian Renaissance feel.

Every tell-tale sign pointed to the fact that this wasn't a place she'd choose to stay on a teacher's salary. She'd have to figure out which almost-maxed-out credit card to put the next few days on. Lisa thought about the air conditioner repair her car needed and mentally moved it back several months on the calendar. Summer in Texas without A/C in her car was going to stink—literally—she'd be a sweating mess—but getting Nana out of here safely came before any creature comforts.

Even though Lisa wished she could find an online coupon and book the smallest room this place offered, as best she could figure out from the conversation between Ryan and the valet, Ryan lived somewhere nearby. He'd said he was playing in a tournament tonight. Surely he didn't afford a residence in all this luxury by gambling?

Based on what he'd said back at the airport, it was more likely that he had some kind of ownership share in this hotel or something equally out of Lisa's orbit.

Whatever he did, Ryan McBride clearly did it well.

Because Lisa was not at Port Provident High School anymore. This was a world of glitz she'd only heard of from others. And she was pretty sure everything about Ryan McBride and Las Vegas was way, way out of her league.

And Nana's too.

Everything in this lobby strengthened Lisa's resolve to get Nana out of this mess and get her the help she needed to make sure she was living out the rest of her years comfortably. Nana had practically raised her and had supported Lisa's long-dimmed Broadway dreams. She deserved to have Lisa looking out for her now. The tables had turned, and it was Lisa's obligation—no, privilege—to take care of the one person who'd never let her down.

Lisa looked at Nana, gently supported by Bill as they caught up to Ryan at the front desk. The older gentleman seemed sincere. And the look on his face at the airport when he took Nana into his arms had been just precious.

But that didn't mean the plans Nana and Bill had apparently made were in either of their best interests.

Nana had always looked out for what was best for Lisa. She'd given sound counsel and wise advice through the years. Lisa could do no less for Nana now.

"We've got everything taken care of, Mr. McBride. You know we'll always do what we can for you, sir."

Lisa made it to the counter in time to watch Ryan place a black American Express Centurion card on the marble countertop. The onyx plastic blended almost perfectly with the surface on which it had been so casually laid.

AmEx Black. Wow. She'd heard about them, but never actually seen one. She didn't play in that league, herself—a charge card given by invitation only, to people with eight figures of net worth and an annual income of more than a million dollars a year.

Quickly, she revised her estimation of Ryan McBride's league.

She wasn't just way, way out of it. She was *way, way, way* out of it.

Like millions upon millions of ways out of it.

"So, we'll be at the Gran Mona Lisa at six-thirty, Russell. That will give my grandfather and his bride here enough time to dine and I can still be at the celebrity thing for the charity tournament by nine-thirty." Ryan tucked the sleek rectangle of black plastic back in his wallet after the man behind the counter swiped it.

Lisa wondered if his wallet would slide back in those form-fitting jeans easily and caught herself staring just a little too long at some of Ryan McBride's more valuable assets in front of her.

She blew out a harsh breath through pursed lips, mentally chiding herself for thinking more about Ryan McBride than her mission to protect Nana. She only had a matter of days to get this straightened out and get Nana on a plane back home—and booked in for a follow-up with the dementia specialist—without a wedding ring in tow.

"Lisa Marie? Are you okay?" Nana's voice brought Lisa back to the here and now.

"Sure, Nana. Just a long day, that's all. Some of us have been up since five-thirty this morning, in another time zone."

"Well, it's five o'clock now," Bill said. "Why don't you ladies go get some rest and get freshened up. We'll meet you at the restaurant for dinner. What floor is it on, Ryan?"

"Fourth. Where are you going until dinner, Pops?"

"I thought I could go back to your place."

Ryan shrugged. "Sure, but it's kind of a long way over to the residence tower. I may live at the Renaissance Grand, but where I live isn't the same as the hotel. I can get one of the guys to get you a golf cart to shuttle you over there."

"I'll be fine, fine." Bill seemed so sure of himself. "And you two, will you be fine?"

Gina Mae absently patted the bottom of her silver curls. "Yes, of course. This is a lovely place."

"What about you, Lisa?"

It was sweet that Bill was so concerned about his guests.

"Well, one question. What's the dress code at this place? Nana packed—I have no idea what's even in this suitcase."

Bill twitched his lip into a thoughtful half-frown. "Well, I don't know. Ryan?"

"For women, cocktail dresses or higher." His eyes looked down and his gaze came to rest on the toes of Lisa's bright yellow sneakers. "The Mona Lisa is the nicest restaurant on the property."

Nana shook her head. "I brought my bright blue dress. I can wear that. But I didn't pack anything fancy like that for you. I just brought that dress you wore to the winter formal at school. I thought it would match the flowers I want for the wedding. I want a big bouquet of roses."

"Is there a place that sells dresses here?" Lisa swallowed, thinking about what kind of shops—and price tags—would be in an ostentatious palace like this.

Her poor credit card. Her poor, plain old green American Express card that was almost to the limit.

Ryan pointed toward the opening to a long, wide hall. "There are shops over there. Look, I'll get Charley to take care of your Nana and my Pops and I'll show you. I need to check on a few things for tonight and the shops are on my way to the elevators."

Lisa hated shopping. Then, she rolled her eyes back in her head as she thought of something she hated even more.

Shopping on a tight deadline.

And an even tighter budget.

In a hotel that clearly didn't know the first thing about affordable.

Especially schoolteacher affordable.

Just one more thing she now needed to sort out, thanks to Nana and her crazy ideas. So far Spring Break was anything but the relaxing time Lisa had planned on.

Keep reading Lucky in Love

Click here: www.books2read.com/LuckyinLoveBook[1]

The Holiday Hearts Series

The Right Resolution[1]
The Cupid Caper[2]
Lucky in Love[3]
May I Have This Dance[4]
First Kiss Fireworks[5]
Falling Forever This Time[6]
Thankful for Love[7]
Mission: Mistletoe[8]

Want to extend your stay in Port Provident?
Start reading the Hearts and Hope Series

Shelter from the Storm[9]
The Doctor's Unexpected Family[10]
His Texas Princess[11]

---

1. http://www.books2read.com/TheRightResolutionBook

2. http://www.books2read.com/TheCupidCaperBook

3. http://www.books2read.com/LuckyInLoveBook

4. http://www.books2read.com/MayIHaveThisDanceBook

5. http://www.books2read.com/FirstKissFireworksBook

6. http://www.books2read.com/FallingForeverThisTimeBook

7. http://www.books2read.com/ThankfulForLoveBook

8. http://www.books2read.com/MissionMistletoeBook

9. http://www.books2read.com/ShelterFromTheStorm

10. http://www.books2read.com/TheDoctorsUnexpectedFamily

Holiday of Hope[12]

Other Books by Kristen

Love Hallmark movies? Pick up Kristen's book October Kiss, based on the Hallmark movie viewers love! Available anywhere books are sold—in paperback, digital, and audio! October Kiss from Hallmark Publishing[13]

---

11. http://www.books2read.com/HisTexasPrincess

12. http://www.books2read.com/HolidayOfHope

13. https://www.books2read.com/OctoberKiss

About Kristen

KRISTEN ETHRIDGE WRITES Sweet Escape Romance—stories with hope, heart and happily-ever-after—for Harlequin's Love Inspired line, Hallmark Publishing, and Laurel Lock Publishing. She's a Romance Writers of America Golden Heart Award nominee and both a Christian Fiction and Inspirational Romance #1 Best-Selling Author.

You can find Kristen in her native habitat—a Texas patio—where she's likely to be savoring the joy of a crispy taco, along with a glass of iced tea. Scents from her essential oil diffuser are also a must, since she's a certified aromatherapist. She's almost convinced her family that it's normal to talk to imaginary people, as long it goes in a book.

Find her online at http://www.kristenethridge.com where you can get a free story for signing up for her newsletter. You can also follow her adventures in writing at www.facebook.com/kristenethridgebooks[1].

Keep up with Kristen by joining her newsletter list[2] and her author pages on Bookbub[3] and Facebook[4]. If you can't get enough of Port Provident, come join the Port Provident Community Center[5] on Facebook, the official gathering place for Kristen and her fans.

www.kristenethridge.com[6]
Facebook[7] Instagram[8]
The Port Provident Community[9] Center
Don't forget...if you love sweet escape romances, join Kristen's newsletter[10]!

1.   http://www.facebook.com/kristenethridgebooks

2.   http://www.kristenethridge.com/newsletter

3.   https://www.bookbub.com/authors/kristen-ethridge

4.   http://www.facebook.com/kristenethridgebooks

5.   https://www.facebook.com/groups/2422381554654795

6. http://www.kristenethridge.com

7. https://www.facebook.com/KristenEthridgeBooks

8. https://instagram.com/kristenethridge

9. https://www.facebook.com/groups/2422381554654795

10. http://www.kristenethridge.com

Acknowledgements

TO THE PEOPLE IN MY life who don't make fun of my tendency to stock up on Valentine's chocolate so I can still eat those crazy chocolate-covered marshmallow hearts well into the summer. Thanks for being my people.

"Love goes by haps; Some Cupid kills with arrows, some with traps"
William Shakespeare, *Much Ado About Nothing*—Act 3, Scene 2

LAUREL LOCK PUBLISHING
Publisher's Note: This is a work of fiction. Names, characters, places, and incidents are a product of the author's imagination. Locales and public names are sometimes used for atmospheric purposes. Any resemblance to actual people, living or dead, or to businesses, companies, events, institutions, or locales is completely coincidental.

Scriptures taken from the Holy Bible, New International Version®, NIV®. Copyright © 1973, 1978, 1984, 2011 by Biblica, Inc.™ Used by permission of Zondervan. All rights reserved worldwide. www.zondervan.com[1] The "NIV" and "New International Version" are

---

1.   http://www.zondervan.com/